ESSENTIAL COLLECTION

The
ESSENTIAL COLLECTION

#1 *New York Times* Bestselling Author

DEBBIE MACOMBER

Marriage of INCONVENIENCE

❤HARLEQUIN®
ESSENTIAL DEBBIE MACOMBER COLLECTION

Recycling programs
for this product may
not exist in your area.

ISBN-13: 978-0-373-47293-2

MARRIAGE OF INCONVENIENCE

Printed in U.S.A.

DEBBIE MACOMBER

is a number one *New York Times* and *USA TODAY* best-selling author. Her books include *1225 Christmas Tree Lane, 1105 Yakima Street, A Turn in the Road, Hannah's List* and *Debbie Macomber's Christmas Cookbook,* as well as *Twenty Wishes, Summer on Blossom Street* and *Call Me Mrs. Miracle.* She has become a leading voice in women's fiction worldwide and her work has appeared on every major bestseller list, including those of the *New York Times, USA TODAY, Publishers Weekly* and *Entertainment Weekly.* She is a multiple award winner, and won the 2005 Quill Award for Best Romance. There are more than one hundred million copies of her books in print. Two of her Harlequin MIRA Christmas titles have been made into Hallmark Channel Original Movies, and the Hallmark Channel has launched a series based on her bestselling Cedar Cove series. For more information on Debbie and her books, visit her website, www.debbiemacomber.com.

To Yakima's Iron Maidens:
Cheryl Nixon, Ellen Bartelli, Joyce Falcon,
Jill Seshiki, Faye and Victoria Ives

One

"I'm so stupid," Jamie Warren wailed, tossing the crumpled tissue over her shoulder. Rich Manning, who was sitting across the kitchen table from her, held out a fresh one. "I trusted Tony, and he's nothing more than a…jerk."

She yanked the tissue from Rich's hand and ingloriously blew her nose. That tissue took the same path as the previous one. "I feel like the biggest fool who ever lived."

"It's Tony who's the fool."

"Oh, right. Then why am I the one sitting here crying my eyes out?" Jamie really didn't expect him to answer. Calling Rich at an ungodly hour, sobbing out her tale of woe, wasn't the most considerate thing she'd ever done, but she had to talk to *someone* and he was the first person who'd come to mind.

He was the kind of friend she felt comfortable calling in the middle of the night. The kind of friend who'd immediately drive over if she needed sympathy or consolation. They'd been close ever since they'd worked together on their yearbook in high school. Although they didn't see each other often, Jamie had always felt their relationship was special.

"At least crying's better than getting drunk, which is what I did when I found out Pamela was cheating on me," Rich admitted with a wry twist of his mouth. He got up and poured them each another cup of coffee.

"You haven't seen her since, have you?"

"Sure, I have. I wouldn't want her to think I was jealous."

Despite everything, Jamie laughed. "You're still dating her? Even *after* you learned she was seeing another guy behind your back?"

Rich shrugged carelessly, as though the entire situation was of little consequence, something Jamie knew not to be the case. Although he'd been devastated, he'd worn a nonchalant facade. He might've fooled everyone else, but not Jamie. His flippant attitude couldn't camouflage the pain.

"I took her to a movie a couple of times," Rich continued. "I played it cool. But as far as

I'm concerned, it was over the minute I heard about that other guy."

"It's over with me and Tony, too," Jamie murmured. Just saying the words produced a painful tightening in her chest. She was truly in love with Tony and had been for nearly a year. They'd often talked about getting married and raising a family together. Jamie wanted children so badly. The weekend before, they'd gone shopping for engagement rings. Her mother, who was crazy about him, had been thrilled. Since Jamie was over thirty her mom tended to worry about her marriage prospects, but even she said that waiting for a man like Tony Sanchez had been time well spent. Sharing the bad news with her widowed mother had been almost as upsetting as learning about the betrayal itself.

"You're *sure* the other woman's baby is his?" Rich asked, reaching for her hand. "She could be stirring up trouble."

"He didn't bother to deny it." In the beginning, Jamie had hoped the woman was lying. She'd searched Tony's face, praying it was all some malicious joke. His beautiful dark eyes had turned defensive, but gradually the regret, the doubt, had shown, and he'd slid his gaze away from hers. It had been a mistake, he'd told her, a momentary slip in judgment. A one-night fling that meant nothing. He felt terrible about it and promised nothing like this would ever happen again.

Tony was cheating on her before they were even married, and Jamie didn't need a crystal ball to know that pattern would almost certainly continue.

"This isn't the first time," she admitted, biting her lower lip to control the trembling. "Margie, in New Accounts, mentioned seeing Tony with a blonde a month or so ago. He'd told me he was out of town and I…I was sure it was just a case of mistaken identity. I should've known then."

"Don't be so hard on yourself," Rich said, bending to brush a wisp of dark brown hair from her temple. "There were plenty of signs that Pamela was playing me for a fool, too, but I was so taken with her—"

"Bust line. Which was always your primary interest."

"That's probably why I never dated *you*," he countered, grinning.

Jamie smiled. The joke was an old one between them. When they'd first been assigned to work together on the yearbook, Rich had been a popular football player and she'd been a nondescript bookworm. They'd clashed constantly. One day, after a particularly nasty confrontation, she'd shouted that if she had a bigger bust, he might actually listen to her. Rich had gone speechless, then he'd started to laugh. The laughter had broken the ice between them and they'd been friends ever since. The best of friends.

"I hear there's help in the form of surgery," he teased, leveling his gaze at her chest.

"Oh, honestly." Her breasts weren't that small, but it was comfortable and easy to fall into their old banter. Focusing on something other than what a mistake Tony had turned out to be provided her with a good—if momentary—distraction. She'd wasted an entire year of her life on him. An entire year!

Rich reached for his coffee, then leaned back in the chair and sighed. "I'm beginning to wonder if anyone's faithful anymore."

"I'm the last person you should be asking that," she said, taking a sip of her coffee. She didn't blame Rich for having doubts. Relationships all around her seemed to be failing. Friends, whose marriages had appeared strong and secure, were divorcing. At work affairs were rampant. Casual sex. Jamie was sick of it all.

"When Mark Brooks cheated on my sister Taylor, she took that teaching position in another state," Rich went on to say. "You know, I never much liked Mark. From the first I felt there was something off about him. I wish I'd spoken to Taylor about it."

"I felt so bad for her."

"The whole family was worried. Then she moved to the backwoods of Montana and a few months later, she married Russ Palmer. Everyone was sure she'd made a terrible mistake, marrying a cowpoke on the rebound, but I've never seen her happier. And now Christy's married to Cody Franklin."

"Christy's married to whom?"

"The Custer County sheriff. She's living in Montana, too."

"But I thought she was engaged to James Wilkens! Good grief, I was at her engagement party just a few months ago."

"It's a long story, but James is out of the picture."

"Christy dumped James?" It was hard to believe. Jamie had assumed they were perfect for each other. They'd acted like the ideal couple at the engagement party, sipping champagne and discussing wedding dates with their families.

Rich chuckled. "If you're surprised by that, wait until you hear this. While Christy was still engaged to James, she was *married* to Cody."

Jamie was shocked. She didn't know Rich's youngest sister well, but she would never have imagined Christy doing anything so underhanded. "I *am* surprised."

"There were mitigating circumstances and it's not as bad as it sounds, but Christy is yet another example of how fickle women can be."

"Women?" Jamie protested. "Men are notoriously untrustworthy—they always have been."

It looked as though Rich wanted to argue. He straightened and opened his mouth, then shook his head. Sighing, he drank the last of his coffee. "I've begun to think commitment means nothing these days."

"I hate to be so cynical, but I agree."

Standing, Rich carried his mug to the kitchen sink. "Are you going to be able to sleep now?"

Jamie nodded, although she wasn't convinced. However, she'd taken enough of Rich's time for one night and didn't want to keep him any longer.

"Liar," he whispered softly.

Jamie smiled and got up, too. He slipped his arms around her and she laid her cheek against his shoulder. It felt good to be held. Rich's comfort was that of a loving friend, someone who truly cared about her without the complications of romance or male-female dynamics.

"You're going to get through this."

"I know," she whispered. But she hadn't been confident of that until she'd talked to Rich. How fortunate she was to have him as her friend. "We both will," she added.

A sigh rumbled through Rich's chest. "Don't you wish life could be as simple now as it was in high school?"

That remark gave Jamie pause. "No," she finally said, then laughed. "I was so shy back then."

"Shy?" Rich argued, releasing her enough to cast her a challenging look. "You were a lot of things, Jamie Warren, but *shy* wasn't one of them."

"Maybe not with you."

"I wish you had been, then you might've done things my way without so much arguing."

"You're still upset that I didn't use your picture on the sports page, aren't you? We've been out of high school for thirteen years and you haven't forgiven me for using that shot of Josh McGinnes instead."

Rich chuckled. "I could be upset, but I'm willing to let bygones be bygones."

"I'm glad to hear it." She led him to the door of her condo. "Seriously, though, I really am grateful you came."

"Call if you need me?"

She nodded. The worst of it was over. She would pick up the pieces of her life and start again, a little less trusting and a whole lot more wary.

Two months later, Rich was sitting in his office at Boeing when the image of Jamie Warren's tear-streaked face drifted into his mind. It was as if their conversation had taken place just the night before—even though he'd talked to her two or three times over the holidays, and she'd sounded good. Cheerful, in fact. Certainly in better spirits than he'd been himself.

She hadn't made any attempt to fool him. Tony had hurt her badly. From what she'd said, he'd made several attempts to resume their engagement, but she'd rejected the idea in no uncertain terms. It was plain to Rich that Tony Sanchez didn't really know Jamie Warren. The woman was stubborn enough to impress a mule. Once she made up her mind, that was it. Oh, she appeared docile and easygoing, but Rich had collided with that stubborn streak of hers a time or two and come away battered and bruised.

It bothered Rich that Jamie had never married. She'd always loved children, and he'd fully expected her to have a passel of kids by now.

Most men, he realized, passed Jamie over without a second glance. That bothered him even more.

The problem, not that *he'd* call it a problem, was that she didn't possess the looks of a beauty queen. She wasn't plain, nor was she unappealing. She was just—he hated to admit it—ordinary. Generally, there was one thing or other that stood out in a woman. A flawless face. Cascades of shining hair, blond or gold or black… Jamie's wasn't blond and it wasn't dark brown but somewhere in between. And it wasn't long, but it wasn't short either. Some women had eyes that could pierce a man's soul. Jamie had brown eyes. Regular brown eyes. Not dark or seductive or anything else, just brown eyes. Nice, but average.

She was about five-five, and a little on the thin side. Giving the matter some consideration, Rich noted that there didn't seem to be any distinguishing curves on her. Not her hips, and certainly not her breasts. He could be mistaken of course, since he hadn't really looked at her that way.... To be honest, he'd never looked at her in any way other than as a friend.

She didn't have a body that would stop traffic. The thing was, a woman could have an ordinary face, but if she had curves, men fell all over themselves. Rich hated to admit something so derogatory about his fellow men, but he felt it was true.

What few took the time to see was Jamie's warm heart and generous spirit. He'd never known a more giving woman. What she'd said about being shy was true, even though he'd denied it. Yet she had spunk and she had spirit. Enough to stand up to him, which was no easy thing.

Pushing against the edge of his desk, Rich rolled back his chair and stood up. He headed down the hallway with determination.

"Bill," he said, striding purposefully into his friend's office. "Got a minute?"

"What's up?"

Rich had never played the role of matchmaker before, and he wasn't sure where to start. "There's someone I want you to meet."

"Oh." Bill didn't look too enthusiastic.

"A friend of mine."

"Widowed or divorced?"

"Single."

Bill's brows arched toward his receding hairline. "You mean a leftover girl."

Rich wasn't comfortable thinking of Jamie as leftover, but this wasn't the time to argue. "We went to high school together."

"High school? Exactly how old is she?"

"Thirty-one." Her birthday wasn't until April. Their birthdays were both in April, and Jamie loved to point out that she was a whole week older.

"She's never been married?" Bill asked, his voice rising suspiciously. "What's the matter with her?"

"Nothing. She's one of the nicest people you'll ever meet."

Bill reached for his In basket and took out a file, flipping it open. "I can't tell you how many times friends—" he paused and glanced up "—*good* friends, have set me up. They always claim the girl's one of the nicest people I'll ever meet. No thanks, Rich."

"No thanks? You haven't heard anything about her."

"I've heard enough."

"What's the matter with you?" It was hard to keep the irritation out of his voice. Bill was thirty-five and twenty pounds overweight, not to mention the receding hairline. Frankly, Rich didn't think his friend had any right to be so damn choosy.

"Nothing's wrong with me."

"I thought you wanted to remarry."

"I do. Someday, when I find the right woman."

"You might well be passing her over this minute," Rich said. "I'm not going to lie to you—she's no Miss America, but she's not ugly, if that's what concerns you."

"Why don't you ask her out yourself, then?"

The question took Rich by surprise. "Well, because...because it would be like dating one of my sisters."

Bill released an impatient sigh. "Why haven't you said anything about her before?"

"She was involved with someone else."

Bill shook his head emphatically. "Forget it. You're a good friend and all that, but I've been set up too many times in the past few years. Frankly, your friend's everything I want to avoid in a woman. She's over thirty and never been married. It doesn't help that she's just out of a relationship, either. I'm sorry, Rich, I really am, but I'm not interested."

Rich found Bill's attitude downright insulting. Before he could stop himself, before he could analyze his actions, he reached for his wallet.

"What are you doing?" Bill wanted to know when Rich pulled out two tickets.

"These are for the Seahawks play-off game against Green Bay. The scalpers are getting three hundred bucks each for these. If you agree to call Jamie for a date, they're yours." His older brother would have his hide for this, but Rich would deal with Jason later.

Bill's eyes rounded incredulously. "You mean you're willing to give me two tickets to the Seahawks play-off game if I go out with your friend?"

"Yup."

Even then Bill hesitated. "One date?"

"One date." But once his fellow engineer got to know Jamie, he'd realize how special she was. In a few weeks, Bill would be looking for ways to repay him for this. Rich would keep that thought in mind when he told Jason he'd *given* away their play-off tickets.

"Someplace nice, too. No pizza in a bowling alley, understand?"

Bill's hand closed over the tickets. "Dinner at the Space Needle followed by an evening at the ballet."

"Good. Just don't *ever* let Jamie know about this."

Bill laughed. "Do I look that stupid?"

Rich didn't reply, but in his opinion, any man who'd turn down the opportunity to meet Jamie Warren wasn't exactly a candidate for Mensa.

"Here's her phone number," he said, writing it on a slip of paper. "I'll give her a call, clear the way, but the rest is up to you."

"No problem," Bill said, pocketing the tickets.

Rich felt downright noble as he returned to his own office. Jamie was one hell of a woman and it was about time someone figured that out. Bill Hastings wasn't nearly good enough for her, but he was an amiable guy. Without too much trouble Rich could picture Bill and Jamie a few years down the road, raising two or three kids.

He felt good about that, better than he'd felt about anything in quite a while.

That evening, Rich went to Jason's apartment on his way home and was relieved to find his brother was out. That meant he could delay telling him what had become of the play-off tickets. It was definitely something he had to do in person, he told himself.

After killing an hour or two at his own apartment, Rich decided to drive over to Jamie's. He rang her bell and waited. It hadn't occurred to him that she might not be home. He was ready to turn away when he heard activity on the other side.

"Who is it?" she called.

"The big bad wolf."

The sound of her laugh was followed by the click of the lock. She opened the door and Rich saw that he must have gotten her out of the tub. She'd hastily donned a white terrycloth robe that clung to her damp skin.

"Rich," she said, surprise elevating her voice, "what are you doing here?" As she spoke, she finished knotting the belt around her waist.

The robe fell open below that, revealing a glimpse of thigh. Rich was having trouble taking his eyes off it and didn't answer right away. His gaze followed a natural progression downward, and he was momentarily astounded to see what long shapely legs she had. Funny, he'd never noticed them before. He grinned, thinking Bill was in for a very pleasant shock.

"Go ahead and finish your bath," he said casually, walking into her kitchen. "I'll make myself at home while I wait."

"I'm almost done."

"Take your time," he called out. He stuck his head inside the refrigerator and helped himself to an apple. He'd just taken his last bite when Jamie returned. As best he could tell, she'd run a brush through her hair and put on slippers. But that was it. The robe rode over her slender hips like a second skin.

"Do you have any plans tonight?" Generally he went out on Fridays, but there wasn't anything he particularly felt like doing that evening.

"Got anything in mind?"

"A movie. I'll even let you choose."

"I suppose you're going to make me pay my own way?"

"I might." He grinned, pleased with himself for coming up with the idea. The suggestion that they attend a movie had been as much of a surprise to him as it obviously was to Jamie. As much of a surprise as offering Bill the playoff tickets...

Actually, it was a damn good idea. This way

he could lead naturally, casually, into the subject of Bill. The last thing he wanted Jamie to think was that he'd arranged anything.

The movie was indeed a stroke of genius, Rich decided as they drove to the theater. He'd always enjoyed Jamie's company and never more so than now. An evening with her was an escape from the games and pretenses involved in taking out someone new—and it was exactly what he needed to settle his nerves. He didn't like to say much, particularly to his family, but Pamela had hurt him badly. He no longer trusted his judgment when it came to women. Oh, he dated. Often. But he was tired of all the games. Pamela hadn't just broken his heart; the damage she'd inflicted went deeper than that. She'd caused him to doubt himself.

Rich pulled into a movie complex in the Seattle suburbs, close to Jamie's condominium. He bought their tickets, but she insisted on buying the popcorn and the chocolate-covered raisins.

He was just thinking how nice it was to be with a woman who wasn't constantly worrying about her weight when she leaned over and whispered, "You ate more than your share of the raisins."

"Do you want me to buy more?"

"No. Just remember you owe me."

It took him several minutes to realize he had no reason to be grinning the way he was, especially since the film was actually quite serious.

"We don't do this often enough," Rich said as they left the cinema two hours later. He meant it, too. He'd been at loose ends for a couple of months but hadn't thought about contacting Jamie. Now he wondered why.

"No, we don't," she agreed, buttoning her coat. She wore jeans and a pale pink sweater. The color looked good on her. He was about to say as much when he remembered the reason for his impromptu visit.

"How about a cup of coffee?" he suggested, linking his arm with hers. There was a coffee shop in the same complex as the theater, and he steered them in that direction.

He waited until they were seated and looking over their menus before he brought up the subject of Bill. "There's someone at work I'd like you to meet."

Jamie didn't raise her eyes from the menu. "Who?"

"Bill Hastings. You'll like him."

"Is he tall, dark and handsome?"

"Yes. No and no."

"Sounds like my kind of man," she joked,

setting aside the menu. The waitress filled their mugs with coffee and Jamie stirred in a liberal measure of cream. "From everything I've heard, it's best to avoid the handsome ones."

"Oh?" He could guess what was coming. He wasn't conceited, but Rich knew he was easy on the eyes—a fact that hadn't gone unnoticed from the time he was in his early teens. Rich had never lacked for female attention, some he'd sought and some he hadn't.

"Yes," she said. "The handsome ones can't be trusted."

"Who says?" Rich demanded, feigning outrage.

"Everyone," Jamie returned without a pause. "They're too impressed with themselves. Or so I hear."

Rich chuckled and, motioning for the waitress, ordered a chef's salad. He felt like having a decent meal for the first time in weeks. He didn't even complain when Jamie stole his olives, claiming it was the least he could do for hogging the chocolate-covered raisins.

Tuesday morning, Bill marched into Rich's office, pulled out a chair and plunked himself down. His face was creased with a heavy frown. "It didn't work."

Rich tried to figure out which project Bill was referring to and came up blank. They were both part of an engineering team working on a Boeing defense contract. Rich had volunteered for this job, knowing it would entail plenty of overtime hours. The challenge was something he needed at this point in his career—and his life.

"What do you mean?" he asked Bill.

"She turned me down flat."

Bill couldn't possibly be talking about Jamie. He'd paved the way for him! He'd managed to casually drop his name into the conversation at least three times. Enough to pique her curiosity, but not so often that she'd suspect he was setting them up.

"She turned you down?" Rich echoed, still unable to believe it. "Obviously you didn't try all *that* hard."

"If I'd tried any harder, I would've been arrested," Bill muttered.

"What the hell did you say to her?"

"Nothing. I called her Saturday afternoon, just like you suggested. I mentioned your name right off and told her we worked together and have for several years. I wanted her to feel comfortable talking to me." He hesitated as though he was still trying to understand what had gone wrong.

"Then what happened?" Rich could feel himself losing patience. He'd risked his brother's wrath by giving up those tickets and he wasn't about to let Bill off so easily.

"That's just it. *Nothing* happened. We must've talked for ten or fifteen minutes and you're right—she sounds nice. The more we talked, the more I realized I wouldn't mind getting to know her. She said you two were on the yearbook staff together.... She even told me a few insider secrets about your glorious football days."

"What the hell were you doing talking about me?" Rich demanded.

"I was establishing common ground."

Rich brought one hand to his mouth in an effort to hide his irritation. "Go on."

"There's not much more to tell. After several minutes of chitchat, I asked her out to dinner. Honest, Rich, I was beginning to look forward to meeting her. I couldn't have been more shocked when she turned me down."

"What did she say?"

"Not much," Bill admitted, his frown deepening. "Just that she'd given up dating and although she was sure I was a perfectly fine guy, she wasn't interested."

"You didn't take that sitting down, did you?"

"Hell, no. I sent her a dozen roses Monday morning, hoping that would convince her. Red roses, expensive ones. I didn't get them in any grocery store, either. These were flower shop roses, top quality."

"And?"

"That didn't do it, either. She phoned and thanked me, but said she still wasn't interested. Said she felt bad that I'd gone to the expense of sending her flowers, though."

Rich muttered under his breath. Bill had just encountered that stubborn pride of hers. Rich knew from experience that once she'd made up her mind, nothing was going to change it. Not flowers, not arguments, nothing.

Bill sighed unhappily. "You aren't going to make me return the Seahawks tickets, are you?" he asked.

Two

Jamie was sitting at her kitchen table, reading the application from the adoption agency, when the doorbell rang. A long blast was immediately followed by three short, impatient ones. By the time she'd stood and walked to the door, whoever was on the other side was knocking loudly.

She checked the peephole. Rich. And from the look of him, he was furious. Unbolting the lock, she opened the door.

Without a word, he marched into the center of her living room, hands deep in the pockets of his full-length winter coat. Damn, but the man was attractive, Jamie noted, not for the first time. Much too handsome for his own good. His blue eyes were flashing, which only added to his appeal—even if they were flashing with annoyance, not laughter or warmth.

"You turned down Bill Hastings's dinner invitation and I want to know why," he said without preamble.

Jamie sighed. She should've realized Rich would be upset about that. He'd obviously gone to a lot of trouble to arrange the date and even more trying to conceal it from her. The seemingly impromptu visit Friday night, the movie and coffee afterward, had all led up to his singing Bill Hastings's praises. He'd listed Bill's apparently limitless virtues at length and actually seemed to think he was being subtle about setting her up.

To be fair, she'd enjoyed talking to Bill. He'd seemed cordial enough, and he had sent her the roses, which really were lovely. But he hadn't said or done anything to change her mind. It did seem rather harsh to turn him down sight unseen, but she was saving them both future heartbreak and disappointment. Bill accepted her decision with good grace, but that clearly wasn't the case with Rich.

"Well?" Rich demanded. He walked around her couch, as though standing still was impossible, but if he didn't stop circling it soon, he was going to make her dizzy.

"He sounds very nice."

"The guy's perfect for you," Rich argued,

gesturing toward her. "I match the two of you up and then you turn him down. I can't believe you refused to even meet him!"

"I'm sorry, but I'm not interested."

"One date," he cried, waving his index finger at her. "What possible harm could there be in one lousy dinner date?"

"None, I'm sure," she said calmly. "Listen, do you intend to stay long enough to take off your coat, or are you just dropping in to argue with me on your way to someplace else?"

"Are you going to let Tony do this to you?" he challenged, disregarding her question. He plowed his fingers through his hair, something he'd done often today if the grooves along the side of his head were any indication.

"Tony has very little to do with this." Rather than discuss the man who'd wounded her so deeply, Jamie moved into the kitchen and poured them glasses of iced tea, which gave her a few minutes to compose her thoughts.

"Obviously Tony has everything to do with this, otherwise you wouldn't have told Bill you'd given up dating. Which, by the way, is the most ridiculous thing I've ever heard." He shrugged off his coat and draped it over the back of a kitchen chair.

"Really?" Leaning against the kitchen

counter, she added sugar and ice to her glass, stirred, then sipped from her tea. Rich ignored the glass she'd poured him.

"It's not true, is it?"

He glared at Jamie as though he expected her to deny everything. But she couldn't see any reason to lie. "As a matter of fact it is."

Rich's jaw sagged open. "Why?"

"You really need to ask?" Jamie said with a light laugh.

"How can you deny that Tony's responsible for this?"

She lifted her shoulders in a shrug. "In part he is, but this decision isn't solely due to what happened with him. It's just one more disappointment. If anything, I'm grateful I found out what kind of man Tony is *before* we were married."

The timer on her oven dinged. Setting aside her tea, Jamie reached for a pot holder and took out a bubbling chicken potpie. The recipe was one she'd come across in a women's magazine and it had looked delicious. True, the meal was large enough to feed a family of four, but she intended to freeze half of it.

"Have you had dinner? Would you like to join me?" She extended the invitation casually as she set the steaming pie on top of the stove to cool.

"No," Rich answered starkly. "I'm not hungry."

"It seems to me you've lost weight. Have you?"

"I'm not here to discuss my weight," he barked, "which hasn't changed since high school, I might add."

His attitude was slightly defensive, but Jamie decided to ignore it. He *had* lost weight; she'd noticed it soon after he'd broken off the relationship with Pamela. Jamie had never met the other woman and it was all she could do to think civilly of her. If anyone was ever a fool, it was Rich's former girlfriend.

"You didn't answer my question," Rich said. His voice had lowered and he seemed less persistent now. Jamie suspected he'd spent the day seething over her decision not to date his friend.

"Which question didn't I answer?" she asked, putting the pot holder back in the top drawer.

"What made you decide to give up dating?"

"Oh." She pulled out a chair and sat down. Rich did, too. "Well, it wasn't something I did lightly, trust me. It was a gradual decision made over the past few months. I honestly feel it's the right one for me. I feel better than I have in years." She tried to reassure him with a warm smile. He was frowning at her as though he wanted to argue. Rich had always been passionate when it came to people he cared about. "I'm nearly thirty-two years old," she added.

"So?"

"So," she said with a laugh, "there aren't many eligible men left for me."

"What about Bill Hastings? He's eligible."

"Divorced, right?"

"Right. But what's that got to do with anything?"

He wasn't going to like her answer, but Jamie wouldn't be less than honest. "I've dated plenty of divorced men over the years. My experience may not be like anyone else's, but I've discovered that if their wives left them, there's generally a damn good reason. And if there isn't, they're so traumatized by the divorce they've become emotional cripples."

"That's ridiculous! And furthermore, it's not fair."

"I'm sure there are exceptions. I just haven't found any."

"In other words, you wouldn't date Bill because he's divorced."

"Not...exactly. It's more than that. I don't want to date *anyone* right now, divorced or not."

"What about single men? You're only thirty-one, for heaven's sake. There are lots of single men out there who'd give anything to meet a woman like you."

Jamie had to swallow a sarcastic reply. If there were as many eligible single men as Rich seemed to think, she certainly hadn't met them. "Obviously I haven't had much luck with that group, either," she said. "I hate to burst your bubble here, but single men aren't all they're cracked up to be. If a man's in his thirties and not married, there's usually a reason for it. Besides, single men over thirty are so set in their ways, they have problems adjusting to the natural give-and-take of a healthy relationship."

"That's downright insulting."

"I don't mean it to be." She stood up to get two plates. "You're having dinner with me, right?"

He nodded.

"I'm not going to lie to you and claim Tony had nothing to do with this," she went on. "He hurt me, and it took me weeks to work through the pain. As strange as it may seem, I'm actually grateful for what Tony taught me. He helped me reach some sound, honest decisions about my life."

"If this no-dating stand of yours is one of them, then I'd do some rethinking if I were you." Rich opened the silverware drawer and took out two knives and forks. Without glancing at the adoption papers, he placed them to one side and had the table set by the time she brought over their plates. Jamie couldn't help being pleased that he'd agreed to join her for dinner.

"My biggest, and probably most significant realization," she said while smoothing the napkin across her lap, "was that I like my life the way it is. I don't need a man to feel complete."

Several minutes passed before Rich spoke. "That *sounds* healthy, but to lock the door on any chance of a relationship—"

"I'm not locking the door," she interrupted, eager to correct that impression. "I'm just not looking for one. I've wasted years trying to fulfill my dream of being married and raising children."

Rich took a bite of the chicken potpie and raised his eyebrows. "Hey, this is great."

"Thank you." She tried it herself and was satisfied with her culinary efforts. Taking the time to cook real meals instead of throwing together a sandwich or resorting to frozen entrées had been another decision she'd reached. It might seem silly, but cooking gave her a feeling of permanence and purpose. She was doing something healthy for herself, and she felt good about it.

"Everything you've said makes sense," Rich admitted reluctantly.

"Don't sound so shocked."

"It's just that I've always pictured you with kids…."

"I've got that covered," she said enthusiastically, removing the top sheet of the papers Rich had stacked on the other side of the table. "I intend to adopt."

"I know they let single people adopt children now," he said, "but two-parent families are better for kids."

"Ideally, yes," Jamie agreed. "But sometimes there's no alternative. Anyway, from what I've read, I don't think it's going to be easy or anytime soon, especially if I want a newborn."

"Which you do?"

Jamie nodded. If she was only going to be

a mother once, then she wanted as much of the experience as she could have, including midnight feedings, teething and changing diapers. "I have an appointment with a counselor at an adoption agency tomorrow afternoon. I haven't been this excited about anything in years."

"I'll bet you haven't told your mother."

Jamie rolled her eyes at the thought. "It's better if I don't say anything, at least for now. Mom's wonderful, but she'd never understand this."

Rich chuckled, but as the laughter drained from his features, his eyes took on a faraway look. "You know what?"

"What?" she asked softly.

"I've basically come to the same conclusion about dating. I'm sick to death of the games and women whose only interest is getting me in the sack. I never knew women could be so aggressive."

Intrigued, Jamie could only nod. She would never have believed Rich was experiencing the same difficulties she had. For years she'd been expecting him to marry, but she'd never felt comfortable enough to ask why he hadn't.

"I've spent ten years looking for a woman who believes love lasts longer than an hour," he added grimly. "As for commitment and honesty, I don't think they exist anymore. Or if they do, then I can't seem to find anyone who believes in them. After Pamela cheated on me I realized I'm a self-reliant adult—and if I never married, it wouldn't make my life any less worthwhile."

"That's how I feel," Jamie said. "I just never thought that—"

"I did, too," he finished for her.

"Exactly."

They exchanged a look—a look wrought with understanding and empathy. They'd been friends for years and Jamie had never known how much they actually had in common.

"I had no idea it was happening to you, too," she whispered. She felt as though she was deprived of oxygen. Everything in the kitchen seemed to fade from view. Everything except Rich. If anything, his dark good looks came into sharper focus. As she had a thousand times before, Jamie acknowledged how very handsome Rich Manning was. But there was much more there, more than she'd ever noticed. This was a man of character and strength. A man of substance. He looked older; the years had marked their passage. There were wrinkles on his forehead and shadows beneath his eyes. The well-defined angles of his cheeks as well as the lines bracketing his mouth only made his face more masculine, more appealing.

The silence between them stretched to embarrassing lengths. It was Jamie who pulled her eyes away first. With a weak smile, she picked up her fork and managed to swallow a bite of her dinner.

"This turned out well, didn't it?" she said in a casual voice.

"Excellent." He seemed equally intent on putting their conversation back on an even keel. He attacked his dinner as though he'd entered a speed-eating competition.

They chatted for several more minutes, teased each other, exchanged the banter that was so familiar to them. Rich insisted on helping her clean up, but as soon as the last dish was put away, he made his excuses and left.

Jamie felt weak afterward. As weak and trembly as the first time she'd stood on the high dive. The feeling wasn't any more comfortable now than it had been all those years ago.

Hard though he tried over the next few days, Rich couldn't forget the look he'd shared with

Jamie at her kitchen table on Tuesday evening. He'd tried to define it, decipher its meaning. It was the kind of look longtime lovers exchanged. The kind he'd witnessed between Taylor and Russ, as though they didn't need words to say what was in their hearts.

But he and Jamie had never been lovers. To the best of his knowledge, they'd never even kissed. *Really* kissed. A peck on the cheek now and then. A friendly hug, perhaps. That was it. Their relationship had always been strictly platonic. It was the way they'd both wanted it. Anything else would have destroyed the special closeness they shared.

Rich shook his head in an effort to banish the disturbing thoughts that had taken up residence there. Until Tuesday, he'd seen Jamie as ordinary. Not anymore.

Still, nothing had changed, not really. At least nothing he could put his finger on. Jamie Warren was the same person she'd always been.

Not so, he corrected. Her eyes had been different.

To think he'd once believed her eyes were an average shade of brown. He'd never seen eyes the precise color of Jamie's. They were a blend of green and brown; some would call it hazel, he supposed. That night they'd been more green, reminiscent of the mist rising off a moss-covered forest floor....

But it wasn't her eyes that had intrigued him. It was something more profound than that. Something more baffling, too.

His musing was interrupted by the phone. Rich grabbed the television remote and muted the volume. He didn't know why he'd bothered to turn it on—from habit, he guessed. For the past hour he hadn't heard a single word of the local or national news. He'd been too busy analyzing what had happened between him and Jamie.

"Hello," he answered briskly. Pamela sometimes phoned him, and he braced himself in case it was her.

"Hi," came the soft feminine voice he recognized immediately as Jamie's.

"Hi, yourself." He felt a bit ill at ease, which he'd never experienced with her. It was as though they hadn't found their stride with each other yet, which made no sense. Perhaps he was taking his cue from Jamie. She didn't sound quite like herself; she sounded tense, as if it had taken some courage to call him.

"I was just thinking about you." He probably shouldn't have admitted that, but it had slipped out.

"Oh?"

"Yeah, I was going to give you a call later and find out how the appointment with the adoption agency went."

She paused, and he heard her take a deep breath. "Actually, that's the reason I'm calling you. Are you busy?"

"Not really. What do you have in mind?"

"Would it be all right if I came by for a few minutes? There's something I need to talk over with you."

"Sure, you're welcome anytime." He glanced around the apartment to see what kind of shape it was in. Not bad. Not especially good, either, but he'd have time to pick up the newspapers and straighten the cushions.

As it turned out, he had time to wipe down the kitchen counter, as well, and stick his dirty dishes in the dishwasher. The best meal he'd had in weeks had been the chicken potpie at Jamie's place. He didn't remember her being such an accomplished cook. She certainly seemed full of surprises lately.

Jamie arrived about ten minutes after her phone call. She wore jeans and the same pink sweater she'd had on the night they went to the movies. He was about to tell her how nice she looked, but stopped himself. Curiously, his heart stopped, too. Just a little.

"That didn't take long," he said instead.

"No… But we only live four or five miles from each other."

"Yeah." He led the way to the sofa and sat down, resting one ankle on the opposite knee and draping his arm along the back. "So, what's up?"

Jamie sat down, too, but he noticed that she sat on the very edge of the cushion and rubbed her hands nervously down her arms. He wondered if she was cold.

That prompted him to say, "Would you like a cup of coffee?"

"Please," she said eagerly.

Rich couldn't shake the impression that she was interested in the coffee more as a delaying tactic than out of any real desire for something to warm her.

He made a pot of coffee, and a few minutes later, brought two steaming mugs into the living room. He had to look around for coasters, but once he found them, he sat down on the recliner across from her and resumed his relaxed pose.

"How'd the appointment with the adoption

agency go?" he asked, when she didn't immediately launch into her reason for the visit. She hadn't really answered his question earlier.

Her hands cradled the mug and she stared into its depths. "Not very well, I'm afraid. Naturally, the agency prefers to place newborns with established families. Besides, the waiting list is years long, and I don't feel I have all that time to wait."

"I'm sorry to hear it." Rich could feel her disappointment.

"If I'm going to have a child, I want to be young enough to enjoy her."

"Her?"

"Or him," she amended quickly, briefly glancing his way.

"So what's next?"

For a long time she didn't say anything. Rich might have grown impatient with anyone else, but he found himself more tolerant with Jamie. He watched the emotions move across her face and tried to read her thoughts. It was impossible to know what she had on her mind, but whatever it was seemed to burden her.

"You're going to think I'm a candidate for intensive counseling when I tell you this."

"Try me."

"I…I've made an appointment with my

gynecologist. I want to discuss the possibility of being artificially inseminated."

Rich was relieved that his mouth wasn't full of coffee, otherwise he would've choked to death. "You're going to do *what?*"

Jamie stood abruptly and walked around the back of his recliner. She braced her hands against the sides as she stood behind him. "I know it sounds crazy, but I plan to have a child, and if I can't adopt, this was the best idea I could come up with."

"What about checking with another adoption agency?"

"I did. Five others, and the story's the same. If I want an infant, it'll mean years on a waiting list. Two of the agencies wouldn't even talk to me. The others tried to persuade me to become a foster parent with the hope of adopting at some point in the distant future. I want a baby. Is that so wrong?"

"No," he assured her gently.

"I'm nearly thirty-two years old, and my biological clock is ticking. Not so loud it keeps me awake nights, but loud enough. If I'm going to do this, it's got to be soon." Jamie's eyes filled with tears, but she was too proud and too stubborn to let them fall. Her gaze met his without wavering. Did she regret being honest because it forced her to reveal her deepest secrets?

"What about the father?" he mumured.

"I…I'm not sure. I've read everything I could find on the subject, which isn't all that much. I understand there's a sperm bank in our area. I don't know what else to tell you, since I haven't been to the doctor yet. I'll have more answers once I've had a chance to talk it over with him."

"I see." Rich could hardly believe they were even having this discussion. "You're positive you want to go through with this?" The minute he asked, he knew he'd made a mistake.

Steely determination shone from Jamie's eyes. "I'm going to do this, Rich, so don't try to talk me out of it."

Her warning wasn't necessary; he was well aware that any attempt to dissuade her would be pointless. "Are you worried about what people might say?" he asked. "Is that what's bothering you?"

She shrugged. "A little. The biggest hurdle will be my mother, but I'm not too worried. It's my life. Besides, she's been after me to have children for years. Of course, she'd prefer it if I were married, but I've decided against that." Her eyes met his again. She seemed nervous, edgy. Rich couldn't remember Jamie being either. Until tonight.

"Something's troubling you."

She closed her eyes and nodded. "You're just about the best friend I have."

"I'm honored."

"I have several close girlfriends. I've been a maid of honor twice and a bridesmaid three times. But when I found out about Tony, it was you I turned to. You're the one I felt I could wake up in the middle of the night."

"I feel the same way about you."

Her smile was genuine, if a little shaky. "That pleases me more than you know. We're good friends."

"Good friends," Rich echoed. Good enough for him to hand over two fifty-yard-line play-off tickets on the off-chance she might find happiness with Bill Hastings. He'd done it without pause, too.

"I'd do just about anything for you," she said, eyeing him closely.

Rich didn't know why he felt that was a leading statement, but he did. The door was wide open for him to echo the sentiment. "You're special to me, too. Do you mind telling me exactly where this conversation is heading?"

Jamie came around the chair and sat on the sofa again. She leaned forward and rubbed her palms together, as though she was outside in below-freezing temperatures. She seemed more sure of herself now.

"You're such a handsome guy."

Rich frowned. "What's that got to do with anything?"

"You come from a wonderful family."

That was true enough. "So?"

"You're tall. What I wouldn't give for an extra two inches."

"Jamie, what the hell are you talking about?"

She stood up, still rubbing her palms. Once more she positioned herself behind his recliner. "I...I was having dinner when it dawned on me exactly what I'd decided to undertake. I want a child and because I do, I'm willing to be subjected to heaven knows what kinds of medical procedures. I don't care. It's a small sacrifice, and I'm amenable to whatever it takes. The only aspect of this entire scenario that disturbs me is giving birth to a stranger's child. A man I've never met, never even seen. Then it came to me. There's one person, a man I admire and trust above all others. It didn't make sense to go through all this and have a stranger's baby when...when there's already someone in my life who's tall, dark and handsome. Someone with excellent chromosomes who might be willing to contribute to this project."

"What are you saying?" Maybe she didn't mean what he thought she meant. Maybe this was all a dream and he'd wake in the morning and have a good laugh. Maybe Jamie wasn't wrong about the counseling. There seemed to be a hundred *maybes* in this. Rich didn't like the answer to a single one of them.

Jamie looked into his eyes and smiled, the softest, sweetest smile he'd ever seen. "I'm asking you to be the sperm donor for my baby."

Three

"Naturally, I don't expect you to make a decision tonight," Jamie added, walking around the recliner and sitting down again. She leaned back and crossed her legs, striking a relaxed pose.

Rich frowned. She sounded so casual, so comfortable with the idea. Mentioning it had obviously demanded courage, but now that her baby plan was out in the open, she seemed completely at ease.

But Rich wasn't. His thoughts were in chaos.

"I...don't know...what to say," he stammered.

"I'm sure the whole thing comes as a shock," she said. "I wish there was some way I could've led up to it with a little more tact, but I couldn't think how to say it other than flat out. I didn't want there to be any room for misunderstanding between us."

Rich was standing now, although he couldn't remember getting to his feet. "No…this is the best way." He paced back and forth in front of the coffee table. "A baby," he muttered, needing to hear himself say it aloud. He was trying to assimilate exactly what it was Jamie had suggested. He paused, waiting to be overwhelmed by objections, but apparently he was too numb to think clearly. Not a single protest occurred to him. Not one.

Questions. There were plenty of those. A few doubts and a whole lot of shock, but no real opposition. Although he'd thought there would be. *Should* be.

"Our baby," she said, her smile serene—as if she was already pregnant and counting the days before their child's birth.

Her attitude, the calm way she was watching him, unnerved Rich more than anything. He stalked into the kitchen, emptied his coffee mug and then refilled it. When he returned, he saw that Jamie was studying him closely.

"Say something." Her confidence seemed to be shaken, and for his own peace of mind, Rich was relieved to see it. She'd been taking this in stride a little too easily.

"I don't know what to say," he admitted bluntly.

"It sounds preposterous to you, doesn't it?"

"Yes," he nearly shouted. *Preposterous* was putting it mildly. She was talking about creating a new life, one that would link them forever.

"Why?"

"Why?" He couldn't believe she'd even ask such a thing. "You want me to father your child. A baby—any baby—is a huge responsibility and—"

"But that responsibility would be mine," she said quickly, interrupting him. "Don't worry, I wouldn't ask for any support, financially or emotionally."

That didn't sit well with Rich, either. He put down his coffee, sank into the chair again and leaned forward, pressing his elbows to his knees. He needed to think but couldn't seem to form a single coherent thought. "Let me see if I understand this correctly," he said after a moment. "You don't want anything from me other than a…biological contribution. I'd father your child, and that's all."

"For this to work, you'd—we'd both need to separate ourselves emotionally from the procedure. The baby would technically be yours, but only because of his or her genetic makeup. For all intents and purposes, the pregnancy and the child shouldn't be any different than if I'd gone to a sperm bank."

"In other words all you really want from me is my genes."

"Yes," she said, nodding emphatically. Her eyes briefly met his, and she appeared to have immediate second thoughts. "I know I'm making it all seem so callous, but that's not my intention. There's no one I trust more than you, no one else I feel comfortable approaching with this idea. If the doctor were to line up ten guys—ten strangers—and ask me to choose one of them to father my baby, I'd pick you instead. Knowing you and trusting you means so much to me. We've been friends since high school and that adds a whole other dimension to this."

"I don't know…."

"I…I considered seducing you."

This time, Rich was unfortunate enough to be in the process of swallowing a mouthful of coffee. It stuck halfway down his windpipe and completed its course only after a bout of violent coughing.

"Are you all right?" Jamie asked.

"You honestly considered seducing me?"

That idea was even more ludicrous than the first one she'd had.

"Briefly," she admitted. "But sex between us would upset everything, don't you think? Your friendship's far too valuable to me to ruin it over something physical."

"I'm glad to hear it." So she'd considered luring him into her bed. Jamie Warren was certainly full of surprises this evening.

"I'm...not sure I could've done it," she said as she lowered her gaze to her hands, which were tightly clenched in her lap. "I mean... well, you know what I mean."

Rich wasn't convinced he did, but he pretended otherwise and simply nodded.

Jamie reached for her coffee and took one tentative sip. "Do you have any questions? I mean, I'm sure you do, and I want to reassure you in any way I can."

"Not yet." He couldn't seem to think clearly, let alone form sensible questions. "You say you're not looking for emotional or financial support?"

"Correct."

"So I'm not supposed to feel anything toward this child?"

Her eyes widened. "I...don't know. I hadn't thought about it in those terms. If it would make things easier for you, I could move out of the area after the baby's born, or...before. Whichever you prefer."

He didn't like that strategy at all. "What about our parents?"

"What about them?" She seemed puzzled.

Rich couldn't speak for Jamie's mother, but he knew his own, and she'd give him an earful the minute she heard about this craziness. "You don't expect our parents to accept this sitting down, do you?"

"I don't plan to tell them."

He gaped at her. "What do you intend to do? Run off and have the baby and then go home and present our parents with a surprise grandchild?"

"My mother, yes, but not yours. I don't intend to tell anyone you're the baby's father. That'll be between you and me. No one else needs to know. As far as my mother's concerned, all I'm going to say is that I was artificially inseminated, but not by whom. That would only complicate matters, don't you think?"

This didn't work any better for Rich than Jamie's other ideas, especially the one about moving away. He rubbed his face, hoping that would help him sort out his thoughts. It didn't.

"I suppose you'll want a few days to think this over?" She eyed him speculatively. It was apparent she'd like her answer as quickly as possible, but that was just too bad. This was too important a decision to be made quickly. He needed to weigh all the concerns carefully, think through the pros and cons.

He found the whole situation unsettling. Sure he'd like to be a father, but he'd prefer that it happened in the traditional way. His first instinct was to reject her suggestion outright, but Jamie was staring at him with those big, round eyes of hers, obviously doing her best not to sway him. To his regret, Rich discovered that he couldn't turn down her request without at least considering it. Their friendship was worth that much.

"Give me a week," he said after a strained minute or two.

"A week," she repeated slowly. "Should I call you or will you call me?"

"I'll call you."

She nodded and stood up to leave, pausing at the front door. "Before I go, there's one more thing I'd like to say."

"Yes?"

"I...I truly believe we'd have a beautiful child, but if it isn't meant to be, then I can accept your decision. I'm going to have a baby. I'd just rather it was yours than some stranger's." With that, she was out the door.

After she'd left, Rich resumed pacing, unable to stand still. His thoughts were a tangle of confused reactions, and part of him was laughing at the absurdity of Jamie's proposition.

Their baby! Their baby?

They'd never even kissed, and she was proposing they create a child together.

She'd told him she expected nothing from him, other than the pregnancy. Although he was sure she hadn't meant to sound so cold and calculating, that was exactly what Rich felt. She'd made it seem so…impersonal. Even that parting shot about having a beautiful child got to him. With those hazel-green eyes of hers and his height… He forcefully pushed the idea from his head.

Although he'd asked for time to make his decision, Rich already knew what his answer would be.

He wanted no part of this craziness.

Jamie made a genuine effort not to think about Rich for the next few days. She'd stated her case, explained what needed to be explained without resorting to emotions.

A hundred times since their talk, she'd thought of all the things she might've said to get him to agree....

Her mind was muddled with regrets. Rich was a good friend. Too good to risk ruining their relationship because she was determined to have a child.

She'd insulted him. She'd known, from his stunned look, that his immediate instinct had been to say no. Good grief, who wouldn't? It was only because of their friendship that he'd been courteous enough to consider her proposal.

Not for the first time, Jamie repressed the urge to call him and withdraw the suggestion. With everything in her, she wished she hadn't said a word. And in the same instant she prayed with all her heart, with all her being, that he'd say yes.

If only she'd approached him differently.

If only she'd told him how much his child would mean to her, how she'd love that child her whole life.

If only she'd assured him what a good mother she was going to be.

If only...

* * *

Rich had made plans to go to his brother Jason's apartment on Sunday afternoon to watch the Seahawks football game. Since Rich had given Bill Hastings their fifty-yard-line tickets, the least Rich thought he could do was bring the beer.

Close to one, nearly an hour late, Rich arrived at his brother's with a six-pack of Jason's favorite beer in one hand and a sack full of junk food in the other.

"About time you got here," Jason muttered when he opened the front door. "The kick-off's in less than five minutes."

"I brought a peace offering," Rich announced, holding up the six-pack. It wasn't like him to be late, and he half expected an interrogation from his brother. He was grateful when it looked as though he was going to escape that. If Jason did grill him, Rich didn't know what he'd say. Certainly not the truth. That he'd been so consumed with indecision over Jamie's proposal, he'd lost track of the time.

"It's going to take a whole lot more than a few beers to make up for the loss of those tickets, little brother," Jason complained as he led Rich to the sofa. "Last I heard, scalpers were getting three hundred bucks for this game, and my brother *gave* ours away." There was more than a touch of sarcasm in Jason's voice. "I still don't understand how Bill Hastings ended up getting *our* tickets."

Rich had been purposely vague about the exchange. "He did me a favor."

"You couldn't have bought him dinner?"

"No." It wouldn't help to tell Jason that the big favor Bill was supposed to have done him had fallen through.

Damn, Jamie was stubborn. Stubborn enough to go ahead and have her baby without him.

That stopped him in his tracks. It was her decision. What bothered Rich, what caught him so completely by surprise, was the rush of resentment he felt at the thought of her having another man's child.

"Hey, you all right?" Jason asked, claiming the seat next to him on the overstuffed sofa.

"Of course I'm all right. Why shouldn't I be?"

"I don't know, but you got this funny look all of a sudden."

Rich dropped his gaze to the can of beer he clutched in his hand. He offered his brother a weak smile and then relaxed on the sofa. It was a few minutes before his heart rate returned to normal. But he kept thinking about Jamie. She'd have a stranger's child. Yes, she would. She'd do it in a second. More than once Rich had collided with that pride of hers, and there wasn't a doubt in his mind.

She'd do it!

"You ever thought about being a father?" Rich found himself asking his older brother. He attempted to make the question sound casual but didn't know if he'd succeeded or not.

"Who, me?" Jason teased. "I'm not even married, and frankly I don't ever plan to be."

"Why not?" This was news to Rich. Jason dated as often as Rich did—although, come to think of it, Rich might have implied that his social life was more active than it really was. Jason never seemed to lack for gorgeous women. The only time he'd gotten serious, the relationship had turned out badly, but that was years ago.

"I'm not the marrying kind," Jason said, tearing open a bag of potato chips with his teeth. "All women think about is reforming me. Hell, if I want to kick off my shoes and watch a football game on a Sunday afternoon, I don't want to feel guilty about it. Most married men are henpecked. I prefer my freedom."

"So do I," Rich agreed. Marriage wasn't for him, either. Or for Jamie. He valued his independence. So did she. Jason apparently felt the same way—marriage was too much trouble.

"If I want to dry my socks in the microwave, there's no one around to yell at me," Jason added, then took a deep swallow of his beer.

"You dried your socks in the microwave?"

Jason shrugged. "I forgot to put the load from the washer into the dryer the night before. I needed a pair for work. So it was either that or pop them in the toaster."

Rich chuckled. That sounded exactly like something his brother would do. Jason was right: A woman would've been horrified had she known about his method of drying socks.

For the next ten minutes they were both engrossed in the game. At the commercial break, Jason propped his ankle on his knee and turned to Rich.

"Why'd you bring up this marriage thing?"

"No reason. I was just wondering."

"What about you?" Jason asked. "Isn't it time *you* thought about settling down and fathering a houseful of kids?"

"Me?" Rich asked.

"Yes, you. Mom knows any future Mannings will have to come from you and Paul. She's thrown up her hands in disgust at me."

"I don't think I'll get married, either."

Jason's eyes widened with disbelief. "Why not?"

"Don't look so surprised."

"I am. You, Richard Manning, are definitely the marrying kind. Women flock to you."

Plainly his older brother had an inflated view of Rich's sexual prowess, and Rich couldn't see any reason to disillusion him. "True, but not one of them, in all these years, has appealed to me enough to want to marry her."

"What about Pamela?"

"That woman's a—" Rich decided not to say it. "Put it this way. We don't have much in common."

"I thought you were still seeing her."

"I do occasionally." He took a swig of his beer and set it down, then reached for a bowl of popcorn. Leaning back, he rested his feet on the coffee table, crossing his ankles. "This is the life." He made a point of changing the subject, growing uncomfortable with the topic of marriage, although he'd been the one foolish enough to introduce it.

"It doesn't get much better than this," Jason said enthusiastically.

Once again their attention reverted to the television. The Seattle football team, the Seahawks, was playing the Green Bay Packers in a heated contest for the National Football Conference title. The winner would go on to play in the Super Bowl. All of Seattle was excited about the game.

"What about kids?" Rich wanted to kick himself the instant the question left his lips. What the hell was the matter with him? He'd had no intention of talking to Jason about any of this.

"Children?" Jason's attention didn't stray from the game. "What about them?"

"If you don't plan to marry, how do you feel about not having a child of your own?" This bothered Rich the most. He really would like a son or a daughter. Or both.

Jason took a long time answering, as though the question had caught him unprepared. "I don't know... I hadn't given children much thought. I guess I'd like a couple of kids someday, but on the other hand, I don't want to get married in order to have them. But then—" he hesitated "—there's no need to marry...

not these days. We live in an enlightened age, remember?"

"Not marry the woman pregnant with my child?" Rich gave his brother a sour look. "I don't care what age we live in. We both know better than that. A word of advice—don't let Mom or Dad ever hear you say such a thing."

Jason exhaled. "You're right, that was a stupid idea." He reached over to the bowl of popcorn Rich was holding and grabbed a handful. "Is there something you're not telling me?"

"Not telling you?"

"Yeah. There's something on your mind."

"I'll tell you what's on my mind," Rich said, picking up his beer. "Football. In case you haven't noticed, we're down by seven points and Green Bay's got the ball on the fifteen-yard line." He laughed, but his brother didn't.

"You're sure?" Jason asked a few minutes later. "The score's the only thing bothering you?"

"Positive," Rich assured him, feigning a smile. A man didn't tell his older brother, especially one who assumed women flocked to him, that he was thinking about becoming a sperm donor.

* * *

Six days had passed, and if Rich didn't call her soon, Jamie was convinced she'd have a nervous breakdown. Every time the phone rang, her heart shot to her throat and she started to tremble like an October leaf.

Rich had made a point of saying he'd be the one to call her, and he'd promised to do so within a week's time. Nevertheless, the wait was killing her, and each day that passed seemed to increase her anxiety.

She'd just put a casserole in the oven when the doorbell chimed. Jamie's gaze flew apprehensively toward the door. Even before she answered it, she knew it was Rich.

Inhaling a deep breath, she walked unsteadily across the carpet and opened the door.

"Hello, Jamie."

"Hi, Rich."

His eyes refused to meet hers, and her stomach twisted into a tight knot as he entered her home. He removed his coat and hung it in the closet as though he intended to stay for a while. Jamie didn't know whether she should take encouragement from that or not.

"Dinner's in the oven. Will you join me?"

He nodded, although she suspected he hadn't heard what she'd said.

"It's a new recipe.... I seem to be in a cooking mode lately. Tamale pie—I found the recipe on the back of a cornmeal box. I've always liked Mexican food."

"Me, too."

"Would you care for some coffee?"

"Sure."

He followed her into the kitchen and sat down at the table. "I suppose you're wondering what I've decided," he said when she brought him his coffee.

It was all she could do not to demand he tell her right then and there. Waiting even one more minute seemed too long. She pulled out the chair across from him and sat down. She was so anxious, her hands were trembling and she clasped them in her lap, not wanting to give herself away.

"I've done a lot of thinking since the last time we spoke," he began.

If the lines around his eyes and mouth were any indication, his thoughts had been serious indeed. It didn't look as though he'd slept much in the past week. For that matter, neither had she.

"I'm sure it hasn't been an easy decision."

"No, it hasn't," he said pointedly. "Before I say anything else, there are a few things I'd like to get straight. Once I do, you may change your mind."

"I'm not going to do that," Jamie said confidently.

His eyes held hers. "Don't be so sure. First and foremost, I want full parental privileges. This child will be as much a part of me as he or she is of you." He spoke forcefully, as though he anticipated an argument.

"What…what exactly do you mean by parental privileges?"

"I want a say in how the child will be raised, as much of a say as you. That means when it comes time to choose a preschool, I'll expect you to confer with me. I don't want you moving out of the area, either. At least not without me being informed and in full agreement, but I can tell you right now, I won't agree."

"Okay," she said hesitantly. The only reason she'd even brought up the subject of moving was to simplify the situation for him. It wasn't what she wanted at all. "Anything else?"

"I'm just getting started. If we go ahead with this, I want visitation rights."

"Of course. I have no intention of hiding the child from you."

"That's not what I understood earlier," he said, frowning.

"I…know. I should have thought this through more carefully before I approached you. I'd come up with the idea of you being the baby's father the same night I talked to you. When I showed up at your place, the idea was only half formed."

Rich seemed cold and distant. It was almost as if they were negotiating something highly controversial and there was no room for friendliness. No room for personal feelings.

"Does that mean you've changed your mind?" he asked.

"No…no, just that I hadn't worked everything out as extensively as I should have before I came to you. It hadn't dawned on me that you'd care one way or the other about the child. I realize now how insensitive that was of me. I apologize for that, Rich, I really do."

"Of course I'd care about the child!"

"I know. If you want full visitation rights, and a say in how the child's brought up, then that's only fair. I have no objections. None whatsoever."

"I'm also going to insist you accept child support."

"But, Rich, that really isn't necessary. I make a decent wage and—" She stopped abruptly at the way his eyes hardened.

"Then the deal's off."

She took a moment to compose herself. "Since that's clearly an important issue to you," she said carefully. "I'll be willing to accept whatever monetary support you deem necessary."

"Emotional support, as well. I don't want you walking the floors at night with a colicky baby."

"What do you expect me to do?"

"Phone me."

He was making everything so much more complicated than it needed to be. "You don't expect me to call you over every little thing, do you?"

"Yes," he said emphatically. "I want all the arrangements between us clear as glass *before* the blessed event. We'll share the responsibilities."

When she didn't respond, he asked, "Having second thoughts yet?"

"Not…really. Is this everything?"

"It isn't." He stood and opened the oven, checking the casserole that was baking inside. He let the door close slowly.

"You mean there's more?"

"One small item."

"One small item," Jamie repeated, assuming she wouldn't have any more trouble with this than his other demands.

"If we do decide to go ahead and have a child together..."

"And I think we should," she said, smiling over at him.

"Fine. Great. Wonderful. If you're sure."

"I'm sure."

"Good. In that case, I insist we get married."

Four

Jamie was too confused to think clearly. Surely Rich didn't mean what he'd just said. It made no sense. "Married...but...you can't be serious."

"I've rarely been more serious in my life," Rich answered, stalking to the far side of her kitchen. He removed two dinner plates from her cupboard and set them on the table. "Naturally, this wouldn't be a conventional marriage."

"Naturally," Jamie echoed, still too bewildered to understand his reasoning. "Then... why are you insisting on a wedding?"

"I want the child to have my name. I don't care if that no longer matters to most people. It matters to me."

"Oh."

"We'll continue to maintain our separate

residences. For all intents and purposes, nothing will change, at least not outwardly. Except that we'll be sharing the care and custody of a child."

Jamie stood in front of the silverware drawer and closed her eyes, trying to force her heart to stop pounding so hard. Rich had made it plain this wasn't any love match—not that she'd ever suspected it would be. Nevertheless, her heart had reacted fiercely to his insistence on a wedding. Because she couldn't help associating marriage with love, despite a great deal of evidence to the contrary.

"What about the pregnancy? I mean…how do you think I should get pregnant?" By the time the question was complete, her voice had dwindled to a whisper.

"You could always seduce me."

Furious, Jamie whirled around and glared at Rich. She could feel the hot blush warming her cheeks, "I should never have admitted that. You're going to throw it in my face at every opportunity, aren't you?"

"No," he denied, but his eyes were sparkling with the blue light of laughter. "I agree with you. Sex between us would ruin everything. I don't want to risk our friendship any more than you do."

The tension eased from between Jamie's shoulder blades.

"We'll need to keep the marriage a secret."

"For how long?" If their child was to have his name, they'd eventually have to tell their families. Jamie wasn't keen on facing her mother with a surprise marriage to go along with a pregnancy. Doris Warren wouldn't take kindly to being cheated out of a wedding any more than Rich's mother would.

"We'd only stay married until the baby's born," Rich explained, revealing no hint of indecision, and certainly no doubts. He apparently had the whole situation worked out to his own satisfaction.

Unfortunately, he'd completely unsettled Jamie. She'd had everything organized and none of her plans included marriage, even a marriage of convenience. The questions were popping up faster than she could ask them.

"What are we going to say after the baby's born?" she demanded.

"That we're getting a divorce."

Jamie felt the sudden need to sit down again. "That we're getting a divorce?" she repeated. Already she could imagine her mother's shock and dismay. Not only would Jamie have married without telling her, but she'd be obtaining a divorce.

"It makes sense once you think about it," Rich continued with matchless confidence.

Maybe it did to him, but Jamie felt as though she were wandering through the dark, lost and confused, bumping into walls she didn't know were there. It had all seemed so simple the night she'd approached Rich.

He pulled out a chair and placed his foot on the seat, resting his right elbow on his knee. "We'll get married at the courthouse as quietly as possible. There's no reason for anyone to know."

"That much I understand.... I'm just not convinced it's necessary."

"I am," he said adamantly.

"All right, all right," she muttered, swiping one hand through her hair. What had seemed such an uncomplicated idea had suddenly taken on more twists and turns than a country road.

"You'll agree to the wedding?"

"I don't know yet."

"Don't sound so enthusiastic."

"I'm not." She sighed loudly.

"As soon as the ink's dry on the marriage

certificate, we can make an appointment with the gynecologist...."

"Good grief, what are we going to tell him?" Jamie didn't relish that task. If Rich wanted to explain why two healthy, normal, *married* adults who wanted a baby would choose such an unconventional method, then more power to him.

"We won't tell him anything. He's a professional—he isn't going to ask a lot of questions. It's none of his business, anyway."

"Rich...I don't know about this."

"If you have doubts, then I suggest you spill them now."

"I'm not sure getting married is the right thing. We don't have to go through a wedding ceremony for the baby to have your name. Couldn't you legally adopt him or her after the birth?"

"Why complicate everything?"

"And marriage *isn't* going to do that?" Jamie cried.

"Marriage will accomplish the same thing now without the legal hassles of adoption later. As I said, it'll be in name only."

"Yes, I know, but..." She hesitated, trying to shape her objections in the form of a reasonable argument. When she spoke, her eyes met his. "You're going to think I'm terribly old-fashioned."

"The woman who asked me to be a sperm donor? Hardly!"

Jamie had the feeling it would take a long time to live that down. "Yes," she said vehemently, "I suppose it has to do with my upbringing, but I've always considered marriage sacred. Somehow, it just doesn't feel right to sneak off and get married and…and then arrange for a divorce nine months later."

Rich was quiet for a moment. "I agree," he finally said, "but this isn't a normal marriage."

"What marriage is?" Jamie asked, thinking of all the friends she'd known over the years who'd married. Each relationship was different from the others. She'd stood by and observed how some couples had grown closer in their love and commitment. Others had drifted further and further apart until it was too late.

"Nothing's going to change, at least not outwardly," Rich tried to reassure her once again. "We're doing this for the child's sake. And for yours."

"For *mine?*"

Rich's eyes narrowed slightly, and when he spoke his voice was cold. "I won't allow your reputation to be damaged by an out-of-wed-lock pregnancy."

That was all well and good, but it was *her* reputation and if she had no objections, then he needn't be concerned. "But Rich—"

"Furthermore," he said, interrupting her. "I refuse to allow my son or daughter to be born a bastard." He raised his hand. "Before you argue with me, I feel the same way about this as I do about the baby having my name. I don't care if it's important to anyone else. It is to me. Besides, why make a kid's life any harder than it has to be?"

"You've got a point," she whispered.

"Still, I can understand your hesitation."

Jamie lowered her eyes. "It's just that I expect you'll want to marry someday. Sooner or later a woman's going to come into your life and this marriage is going to complicate everything for you. What are you going to tell her about me—and the child?"

"The truth."

"But Rich—"

"It's not going to happen. If I believed I was eventually going to marry, I wouldn't have agreed to this."

Any doubts Jamie entertained were wiped out with the certainty of his smile.

"So you'll marry me?" he asked.

Jamie nodded. She still wasn't convinced it was the right thing to do, but he'd insisted on it so she felt she had no choice.

"One last thing," Rich said, placing his foot back on the floor.

There was *more?* Jamie's head was still reeling from his last announcement. "Now what?"

"You're important to me. Our friendship's important. For the sake of that friendship, I think we should have everything drawn up legally. I don't want any misunderstandings later on."

This seemed logical to Jamie. "Okay, but most of the lawyers I know through work handle real estate and wills and business mergers. This isn't their kind of contract."

"I know an attorney who'll do it. One I trust."

"Who?"

"James Wilkens, Christy's ex-fiancé."

James Wilkens's office reminded Rich of his youngest sister, Christy. She used to work here, and he'd stopped by a couple of times over the past year to take his sister to lunch. He half expected her to come around the corner at any moment.

Christy was married to Cody, however, not James. Sheriff Cody Franklin. Rich wasn't likely to forget how he'd interrupted their wedding night, nor was Cody going to *let* him forget it. Rich had arrived at her apartment soon after he'd found out about Pamela's little fling. He'd been disgusted and disheartened, convinced women didn't know the meaning of the word *faithful.* He hadn't included Christy in that, though. Not his little sister; she'd always been so sweet and virtuous. Then, not knowing they were married, he'd stumbled upon her in bed with Cody, and his opinion of women had fallen to an all-time low.

Sitting in the plushly decorated waiting room next to a five-foot potted philodendron brought back an abundance of memories. The plant was on one side of him, with a fidgeting Jamie on the other.

He glanced at her. She was flipping through the pages of a magazine so fast she'd created a draft. She was on her third issue of *Good Housekeeping* and they hadn't been seated for more than five minutes.

She remained ambivalent about the idea of marriage, but she wanted the child enough to agree to his terms.

Unlike Jamie, Rich felt comfortable with

the plan, for all the reasons he'd given her. He wasn't sure what anyone else would think, especially his family—if they ever found out—but frankly that was their problem. He was doing his best friend a favor.

Rich had the almost overwhelming urge to laugh. Never had he thought he'd agree to anything like this. According to Jason, women gravitated naturally toward him. In some ways that was true, but they were usually the wrong women. What he wouldn't give to have fallen in love with a woman as genuine and compassionate as Jamie.

The need to touch her, to reassure her, even in the smallest of ways, was as strong as the urge to laugh had been a few minutes earlier. He reached for her hand, entwining her fingers with his own.

She looked up at him. "I'm sorry."

"For what?"

"I...I can't seem to sit still."

"We aren't at the courthouse, you know. This is a meeting with James. He's a decent guy, and a darn good attorney. He isn't going to laugh or make snide remarks."

"I know.... It's just that..." She let the rest of the sentence fade.

"You're nervous."

"I'm nervous," she said. "I don't understand why, exactly, but my stomach's in knots and I can't seem to read, and I keep thinking of everything that could go wrong."

"Like what?"

Jamie turned from him and stared down at the open magazine in her lap. "I… You wouldn't understand."

"Try me."

"Marriage shouldn't be taken lightly. I know I've said that before, but I can't seem to explain it in a way that you'll understand. Something happens to a couple when they marry—even when it's only a marriage of convenience. Something…spiritual. I know you don't agree with me, but we're both going to be affected by this. I can't shake the feeling that deep down we'll regret it."

"We aren't going to have a physical relationship."

"I know all that," she said, "but it doesn't change what I feel."

Her hand was trembling in his, and he could tell from the way her voice quavered that she was close to tears. "Do you want to call it off?" Rich would accede to Jamie's wishes, but he hoped she wouldn't back out now.

"That's the crazy part," she said, her expression even more anguished than before. "I want this marriage and our child more than I've ever wanted anything in my life."

"So do I," Rich admitted, realizing how true it was. "So do I."

"Rich," James greeted him as he came into the waiting room. Rich stood and they exchanged handshakes. "It was a pleasant surprise to find your name on my appointment calendar this morning." The attorney looked from Rich to Jamie, and he smiled warmly.

"This is Jamie Warren," Rich said.

"Hello."

"We met briefly...a while back," she said, suddenly biting off her words. She cast an embarrassed glance at Rich, as though she'd made a dreadful blunder. Fortunately James didn't react at all. It wasn't until they were inside James's office that Rich remembered the two of them had been introduced at James and Christy's engagement party.

"Come on in and sit down," James said, motioning toward the two upholstered chairs positioned on the other side of his desk. James, who was of medium height with broad shoulders and a hairline just beginning to recede, had a rather formal manner and a natural reserve.

Rich knew from mutual acquaintances that he'd taken the broken engagement hard. He'd loved Christy and been deeply wounded when she'd married Cody instead. Rich had heard that James rarely dated. If so, that was a shame. James had a lot to offer a woman. He was a junior partner with the firm these days and his talents were in high demand. It would take one hell of a woman to replace Christy, and Rich could only hope that James would find someone just as special.

"So," James said, reaching for his pen and a yellow pad, "what can I do for you?"

Rich leaned back in his chair. "Jamie and I would like you to draft a prenuptial agreement."

The attorney's gaze flew to Rich's. "Congratulations! I'm delighted to hear it. I didn't know you were engaged."

"We aren't…exactly," Jamie said hurriedly. When James focused his attention on her, she shifted in her chair and gestured at Rich. "You'd better explain…everything."

"This will be a marriage of convenience," he announced.

"A marriage of convenience," James echoed, as though he wasn't sure he'd heard correctly.

"There are…extenuating circumstances."

"We're going to have a baby," Jamie inserted, then as she realized what she'd implied, her eyes grew wide. "I'm not pregnant, at least not yet, but if everything goes according to schedule, I will be in the next couple of months."

James lowered his pen. "This doesn't sound like a marriage of convenience to me."

"We aren't going to destroy a perfectly wonderful friendship by having sex," Jamie declared vehemently, slicing the air with her hands. "We agreed on that first thing."

The pen was carefully placed on the polished mahogany desk. James frowned at Rich, then cleared his throat. "Let me see if I understand this. You plan for Jamie to become pregnant, but there isn't going to be any sex?"

"Before we go any further, I want the details of the divorce clearly spelled out," Jamie added, sliding to the edge of her cushioned seat. She slipped her hands under her thighs, but continued to fidget, crossing and uncrossing her ankles. "They should be as explicitly drawn up as the particulars of the marriage. And by the way, we won't be living together. But that shouldn't matter, should it?"

"You're planning the divorce now?" This

time, James made a few notations on the pad, frowning again.

"You don't expect us to stay married after the baby's born, do you?"

"Rich?" James gave him a stern look. "Would you kindly explain what's going on here?"

"We're getting married, having a baby and getting a divorce. A, B, C. Points one, two, three. It's not nearly as complicated as it sounds." Rich found he was enjoying this. James, however, obviously wasn't.

"A prenuptial agreement—okay, fine. We have several forms already drawn up that you can read over. The two of you can decide which one suits you best and amend it as you see fit. But—"

"But what about the baby and the divorce?" Jamie asked nervously. Turning to Rich, she added, "I don't think James understands what we're planning."

"You're right about that. The marriage I understand—at least I think I do. Unfortunately it's everything else that's got me confused."

"There's a logical explanation for all this," Rich assured him.

"No, there isn't," Jamie said sharply. "Rich insists we marry and I don't feel it's necessary, but nothing I say will convince him. If I didn't want a baby so much, I'd never agree to this."

"Rich?" Once again, James looked at him, clearly more baffled than ever.

"It's not as confusing as it seems," Rich told him a second time. "A bit unconventional, perhaps, but not confusing." He spent the next ten minutes explaining their plans and answering a long series of questions from the attorney.

"It sounds crazy, doesn't it?" Jamie said when Rich had finished. "You probably think we both need appointments at a mental-health clinic. I don't blame you, I really don't."

James took his time answering. He continued making notes, then raised his head to look pointedly at Rich. "Are you *sure* this is what you want?"

"I'm sure." Rich shared few of Jamie's concerns regarding the marriage. It was merely a formality. She kept talking about it as though it were a deep spiritual experience. For some couples, marriage might well be that. But not for Jamie and him.

"What about you, Jamie?"

Her head came up sharply.

"Are you sure this is what *you* want?"

She hesitated, then nodded emphatically. "I'm sure."

James paused, rolling the pen between his open palms as he collected his thoughts. "Does your family know about your plans?" The question was directed at Rich.

He gave a short, scoffing laugh. "You've got to be joking. I don't intend to let them find out, either. At least not right away. They'll learn about the marriage and the baby eventually—that much is inevitable. But the longer I can keep this from my parents, the better."

"On that, I can agree."

"So you'll write up an agreement for us?" Rich asked. He hadn't missed the subtle note of concern in James's voice.

"I'll have one drawn up within a week."

"Good." Rich took Jamie's hand. They both stood, and she tucked the long strap of her purse over her shoulder. "Then we'll go off to the courthouse now and apply for the wedding license."

"Might I offer you two a bit of advice?" James asked, standing himself. He rubbed the side of his jaw as if he hadn't decided exactly what he wanted to say.

"Please." Jamie's tone suggested that she hoped someone would talk her out of this scheme. If that was the case, Rich would be the first to remind her that she was the one who'd started the whole thing.

"I'll write up whatever you want me to," James said thoughtfully, "but I don't believe there's any reason to rush into anything. You've both waited this long to have a family—a few more months isn't going to make any difference."

Rich looked to Jamie for confirmation, but he couldn't read her thoughts. "We'll talk about it," he promised.

James nodded. "I'll give you a call later in the week and you can stop by and read over the agreement."

"Great." Rich steered Jamie toward the door, although she didn't need any encouragement. She seemed downright eager to escape. "I'll be talking to you soon then," Rich said over his shoulder.

"Soon," James promised.

Jamie was quiet on the way to the parking lot. For that matter, so was he. Although James Wilkens hadn't explicitly stated his misgivings, they were all too apparent—from the questions he'd asked and the hesitation Rich had heard in his voice.

Rich unlocked the passenger door and held it open for Jamie. He waited until she was inside, his hand on the frame. "Do you want to take some time to think this over?"

"No," she said instantly. "Do you?"

He shook his head. "No."

Their eyes met and held until they were both smiling broadly.

Rich woke early Tuesday morning, before the alarm went off. He turned on the shower and stepped under the plummeting spray, enjoying the feel of it against his skin. He was whistling cheerfully when the tune slowly faded, one note at a time.

He quickly finished showering, reached for a towel and headed directly from the bathroom to the phone at his bedside. He punched out the number from memory and waited impatiently for Jamie to answer.

"Good morning," he said enthusiastically.

"Good morning," came her groggy reply.

"You know what today is, don't you?"

"Of course I do. It isn't every day a woman gets married."

"Second thoughts?"

"Third and fourth if you want the truth, but now that I've had a chance to think it over, I'm more certain than ever."

"Good." He'd grown anxious in the shower,

convinced Jamie would change her mind at the last minute. He had to be assured one final time, although they'd talked of little else in the past week.

James had contacted him Friday afternoon, and Rich had stopped at the attorney's office on his way home from work. The agreement was several pages long, but when he asked for the bill, James had insisted it was a wedding present. The gesture took Rich by surprise. James was the only person who knew what they intended, and he was acting as though this was a conventional marriage. Of all people, James was well aware exactly how unconventional it was going to be.

"You think we're nuts, don't you?"

"No," James had responded with a wry grin. "I think you're both in love and just don't know it yet."

James's comment had caught Rich off guard. He would never have taken the attorney for a romantic.

I think you're both in love and just don't know it yet. On this, the morning of his wedding, Rich tested James Wilkens's theory once again. Sure, he loved Jamie, but not in the sense James implied. They were friends. Pals. Not lovers. Not soulmates. Just friends.

"Have you arranged for a witness?" Jamie asked, pulling Rich out of his reverie.

"A witness?"

"Rich—" she groaned "—don't you remember? When we applied for the license, we were told we'd each need to bring a witness. What do you plan to do, drag in someone from outside the judge's chambers?"

Rich thought about it for a moment. "I suppose so."

"Don't forget the ring," she said, beginning to sound nervous.

"I won't."

"As soon as the ceremony's over, I'll return it." Rich intended to use a small diamond that had once belonged to his grandmother. Jamie had objected, until she'd hit upon the idea of returning it after the ceremony. Wearing a diamond would raise too many questions, she'd decided. The only reason they even needed one was for the exchange of vows.

"Who's going to be your witness?"

Jamie paused. She couldn't very well ask any of her friends. "I...I'm not sure yet. I was thinking of Margie from New Accounts. Margie can keep a secret. But then I thought it might not be a good idea if anyone from the bank knew I was getting married."

"What do you plan to do?" he asked, mimicking her words. "Drag in someone from outside the judge's chambers?"

"I suppose so," she returned, and laughed. It had been at least a week since Rich had heard her laugh. It encouraged him, and he chuckled, too.

"You haven't heard from anyone?"

"No. You?"

Their biggest concern was that one or more of their family members would somehow find out that they'd applied for a marriage license.

In his worst nightmare Rich could envision his mother sobbing hysterically, interrupting the ceremony. She'd be furious that he was marrying Jamie without the large church wedding she'd looked forward to having for Taylor and Christy. Both of Rich's sisters had chosen small private weddings without any family present. For that matter, so had Paul. And he was doing the same thing.

The family honor now rested in Jason's hands.

Jason.

"Rich." Jamie's voice cut into his thoughts. "Don't worry, I'll have a witness."

Rich got dressed in a hurry, his movements filled with purpose.

He grabbed his raincoat on his way out the door and found himself whistling once more as he unlocked his car. He checked his watch and realized he had plenty of time. More time than he knew what to do with.

He drove to his brother's veterinary hospital in the south end of Seattle. There he saw three people in the waiting room. Two in the section marked Dogs and one little old lady clinging tightly to her cat on the other side of the room.

"Is Jason in?" he asked the receptionist.

"He's with a Saint Bernard, but he'll be out soon."

Sure enough, Jason appeared five minutes later. He wore a white lab coat, but underneath, Rich knew he had on jeans and a T-shirt.

"Rich, what are you doing here?"

"Can you take an hour off later today?"

"You buying me lunch?" Jason asked.

"No. I need you to be the best man at my wedding."

Five

Jamie was at the courthouse at the agreed-upon time, pacing the corridor outside Judge Webster's chambers. Ten to two.

She was there, but Rich wasn't.

If he left her standing at the altar—so to speak—she'd personally see to his tar and feathering.

She called his cell phone. No answer.

For the tenth time, she checked her watch.

Seven minutes late. The man would pay for this.

A woman Jamie assumed was the judge's secretary stepped into the hallway. "It's almost two. The judge can see you now."

"Ah…hello," Jamie said, giving the middle-aged woman her brightest smile. "My… The man I'm going to marry seems to have been detained. I'm sure he'll be here any second."

"I see." She glanced at her watch as though to say the judge was a busy man.

"I'm sure he'll be here," she repeated. A slow death would be too good for Rich Manning if he wasn't. "I was wondering…when Rich does arrive, would it be possible for you to be my witness?" She shouldn't have left it to the last minute like this, but she hadn't known who to ask.

"Of course." The gray-haired woman returned Jamie's smile. "Let me know as soon as your young man shows up."

"I will, thank you."

Jamie tried his cell again, and again he didn't answer. She resumed her pacing. She'd made the mistake of asking for the whole day off. If she'd only taken half a day, she wouldn't have all this time to contemplate what she was doing. In the last five minutes she'd vacillated between thinking marriage was the best solution and feeling convinced that it was the most foolish decision she'd ever made.

"Jamie." Breathless, Rich came around the corner at a half run.

"Where have you been?" she cried, her voice cracking under the strain. She was caught halfway between abject relief and total fury. Halfway between hope and despair, trapped in a world of nagging questions and second thoughts.

Rich pulled her into his arms and hugged her close. His breathing was labored, as though he'd raced up several flights of stairs. "I got stuck in traffic."

Jamie was about to chastise him for not allowing enough time, but she swallowed her irritation. What did it matter? He was there now. Suddenly she felt a relief so great all she wanted to do was wrap her arms around him and weep.

"Judge Webster's secretary said we should go into his office as soon as you arrived," she said, composing herself.

"Just a minute. We have to wait for my witness," Rich said, smiling down at her. His beautiful blue gaze was filled with a teasing light.

"You actually brought someone with you? Who?"

"Me," Jason Manning said, hurrying around the same corner Rich had a moment earlier. He, too, was out of breath. "Rich left me to park the car," he said, pressing his hand over his heart. "Said if he was late for his wedding, you'd skin him alive."

"He was right, too."

Jamie's gaze flew to Rich, whose expression was both tender and amused. He'd brought family! They'd discussed the subject at length and had agreed not to let any of their immediate relatives in on their plans. Not until it was necessary, which they'd calculated would be when Jamie entered the fifth or sixth month of her pregnancy.

"Bringing Jason seemed like a good idea at the time," Rich said with a chagrined look. "He spent half the morning arguing with me. According to Jason, we're both candidates for the loony bin."

"We weren't going to tell anyone, remember?" They'd decided that the fewer people who were in on this, the better. But at the rate Rich was telling people, Jamie wouldn't be surprised to see her picture splashed across the front of a grocery-store tabloid.

"Don't worry," Jason inserted smoothly, "I've been sworn to secrecy."

"I'll explain everything later," Rich promised in a low voice. He draped his arm over her shoulder and inhaled noisily, as though he still needed to catch his breath. "But right now, we've got a wedding to attend."

Jamie knew the ceremony itself wouldn't last more than a few minutes; she'd taken comfort in that. They'd be in and out of the judge's chambers in five minutes, ten at the most.

They stood before Judge Webster, their backs stiff and straight. The judge attempted to reassure them with a smile.

Jamie needed to be reassured. Her knees were shaking, her hands trembled and she wasn't sure she'd be able to go through with this.

When it came time to repeat her vows, she hesitated and raised her eyes to Rich. How could she promise to love him and honor him for the rest of their lives, knowing full well their marriage wouldn't last the year?

Rich must have read her confusion and her fears. Some unfathomable emotion flickered in his eyes, and she wondered if he was experiencing the same doubts. When his hold on her hand tightened, Jamie was grateful. She felt the need to be close to him. She didn't know why, any more than she understood the reason she'd agreed to go through with this wedding ceremony.

When she spoke, her voice shook, then steadied and grew strong. Her heart was pounding, then gradually returned to a normal, even beat. She realized that the calmness she felt, the serenity, had come from Rich. His eyes didn't leave her, and his own voice was confident and sure.

They exchanged rings, his hand holding hers as he slipped the delicate diamond that had belonged to his grandmother onto Jamie's finger. He revealed no hesitation. Once the ring was secure, her gaze slowly traveled up to his face. She stopped at his eyes, so blue and clear. They were just as steady as his hand.

The judge pronounced them husband and wife, and with a naturalness Jamie didn't question, Rich drew her into his embrace. Her hands gripped his shoulders as he lowered his mouth to hers. To the best of Jamie's memory, this was the first time they'd kissed, *really* kissed.

Rich made it worth the wait.

His mouth slid possessively over hers, coaxing open her lips. His own were warm and moist, gentle and teasing, giving and demanding.

Jamie was overwhelmed by the variety of sensations he evoked. She felt light-headed and giddy. Appreciated and adored. It seemed that her entire world had been inadvertently turned upside down and she was groping to find her balance.

She shouldn't feel this way, she told herself. She shouldn't be feeling *any* of these sensations. Rich didn't love her—not like this. Nothing like this. One kiss, and he made her feel as though she'd never been kissed before, as though she'd never experienced love before.

Maybe she hadn't. Maybe this was all in her imagination, her mind creating a warm romantic fantasy in order to appease her conscience. Maybe this was a subconscious effort to wipe out the ambivalence she'd felt during the ceremony.

The sound of Rich's older brother clearing his throat brought Jamie back to reality. Rich—her husband—reluctantly let her go and just as reluctantly turned his attention to Judge Webster. The two men exchanged handshakes.

"Thank you so much for being my witness," Jamie said to Judge Webster's secretary. She never did catch the woman's name.

"I was pleased to do it," the secretary told her. She stepped forward and gave Jamie an impulsive hug. "The judge marries a number of couples every year, but I have a good feeling about you and your young man. I think you two are going to be just fine."

Jamie didn't know what to say. She felt like the biggest phony who'd ever lived. It was happening already—the very thing she'd tried to warn Rich about. The feeling of connection. She'd sensed it during the ceremony and even more so with his kiss. But their marriage wasn't supposed to be about any kind of spiritual or emotional connection. It was supposed to be a convenience, a legal shortcut to giving Jamie what she wanted—a child.

They were making a mockery of everything marriage was meant to be. Jamie had never felt more like crying in her life.

She'd tried to convince herself they were doing the right thing. Rich was so confident, so certain, and she believed him because… because she'd always believed him.

But if they were doing what was right, why was her stomach in knots? Why did she feel as though she was going to burst into tears? And why, oh why, had Rich kissed her the way a husband kisses his wife—the most cherished wife in the world?

"Congratulations," Jason said, moving toward her.

She tried to smile, but her mouth started quivering and tears fell from the corners of her eyes, running down the sides of her face.

"Jamie?" Jason asked, giving her a hug. "Are you okay?"

"No."

Jamie didn't know how Jason managed it, but within minutes they were out of Judge Webster's chambers and Rich was at her side, his arm around her middle.

"All right," he said gently, guiding her down the hall, "why the tears?"

Jamie rubbed her hand across her cheeks, suspecting she'd smeared mascara over her face in the process. She'd dressed so carefully in her new pale pink suit. Like a romantic fool, she'd had her hair styled and nails manicured—and for what? So she could stand before God and man and say vows they'd never be able to keep.

"You honestly want to know what's wrong?" she wailed, snapping open her purse and rummaging around for a tissue. She found one, tucked her handbag under her arm and noisily blew her nose. "You mean you haven't guessed?"

"No."

"I...I feel dreadful."

"Why?" Rich looked completely bewildered.

"Because I just lied."

"Lied?"

"So did you!"

"Me?" He sounded even more confused.

"How can you justify what we did? We stood before Judge Webster and said vows. Vows! Vows are serious. We made promises to each other, promises neither one of us intends to keep."

"I can't speak for you, but I certainly intend to honor my vows."

"Oh, right," Jamie muttered sarcastically, rubbing her hand beneath her nose. "You're going to love me in…in sickness and health and everything else you said."

"Yes." Rich didn't so much as blink.

"How…can you?"

"True, this might not be a traditional marriage. Nevertheless, it is a marriage. And like I said, I fully intend to honor every promise I made for the full duration of the marriage."

"You do?" she asked on the tail end of a sniffle.

"You mean you don't?"

"I…I suppose so. It's just that I hadn't thought about it like that. I do love you, you know…as a friend."

As Rich walked her toward the elevator, his hands were clasped behind his back and his head was bent. Ever diplomatic, Jason remained a few steps behind them. "The problem," Rich said, "is that we've each put years of effort into finding the perfect mate. We've spent years looking for that special person—someone we'd be willing to commit the rest of our lives to—but neither of us found what we were looking for. So when we stood before Judge Webster…" He hesitated as though he'd lost his train of thought.

"What we were pledging…the seriousness of our decision hit us hard," Jamie finished for him.

"Exactly," Rich agreed, nodding.

"Then you felt it, too?" She stopped walking and turned to face him, her heart in her throat. Rich had experienced the same reaction she had while they were repeating their vows. He, too, had felt the solemnness of it all.

"I did…very much," he whispered. "A wedding ceremony is a sobering affair. If you didn't understand it before, I want to make it clear now. I'm committed to you, Jamie. That commitment will be the same for the baby once he's born."

"Or she," Jamie murmured, gnawing on her lower lip. Rich *had* said as much before, only she hadn't understood it. He planned to provide financial support for their child and emotional support for her. He'd also insisted they marry so the child would bear his name.

But she hadn't thought of that as a commitment until he'd put it in those terms. A sense of contentment stole through her.

They continued walking side by side, toward the elevator, which was at the far end of the corridor. Rich matched his stride to hers. He was several inches taller than Jamie, and every once in a while, his shoulder would brush against her. His touch felt intimate and special. Jamie was sure he didn't intend or expect her to feel anything at his touch, but she did. She couldn't help herself.

"It's going to be all right, isn't it?" she asked when they stopped to wait for the elevator.

"Not if our parents find out, it won't be," Jason answered for Rich.

"They won't anytime soon unless you tell them." There was a clear warning in Rich's words.

"Hey," Jason said, raising his right hand. "I've already promised not to say a word—to anyone. Mom and Dad would have to torture it out of me."

Rich chuckled and slowly shook his head. "All Mom would need to do is offer you homemade bread fresh from the oven."

"Maybe so. But be aware that the fur's

gonna fly once she learns she missed out on another one of her kids' weddings."

"She'll adjust," Rich said, looping his arm over Jamie's shoulder.

"Are you as full as I am?" Rich asked, leaning back against the upholstered circular booth. His hands rested on his flat stomach and he breathed in deeply.

"I couldn't eat another bite if I tried."

Rich had made reservations for their wedding dinner at the restaurant on top of the world-famous Space Needle. He'd planned every aspect of their wedding-day celebration, from the matinee tickets he'd purchased for a musical at the Fifth Avenue Theater, to a special dinner.

"What did Jason mean when he said you kidnapped him?" she asked. Not that it really mattered, she thought, basking in the pleasures of the most memorable day of her life.

Rich reached for the wine bottle and replenished both their glasses. "To be honest, I did kidnap him. Why…is another story. I'm not sure myself, especially when I knew he'd try to talk me out of this."

"He did try, didn't he?" That went without saying.

"Not at first." Rich arched a brow as though he was still a bit surprised by that. "He actually seemed excited—until he heard the full details."

Jamie groaned. "You told him…everything?"

"He's my brother." Rich picked up his wineglass and sipped. "When I first told him about you and me, he was thrilled. He said he's always admired you and felt I couldn't have made a better choice."

"He said that?" Jamie couldn't help feeling a little incredulous. She barely knew Rich's older brother. Oh, they'd met on several occasions, but the longest conversation they'd ever had was at Christy's engagement party, and that couldn't have lasted more than five minutes. Jason had been miserable in a suit and tie, and kept edging his finger along the inside of his collar. Actually, Jamie had spent more time that night talking to Jason than she had to Rich. Her now-husband had escorted some blonde to the elegant affair, and the woman had stayed glued to his side all evening.

A surge of irritation flashed through her. She'd never been keen on Rich's choice of girlfriends. She swore he could spot a bimbo a mile away.

He attracted them—and he attracted *her*.

That was a brand-new perception, a brand-new awareness.

Until he'd kissed her in the judge's office, Jamie had never thought of Rich in a physical way. He'd always been attractive, too handsome for his own good. But what she'd experienced earlier that afternoon had nothing to do with his looks. Instead, it had a whole lot to do with sensuality.

Rich made her feel vulnerable. Exposed. Powerless. And yet…powerful, too. Everything, all the emotion, all the sensations, had come rushing toward her at once.

Afterward, he'd been so concerned. So understanding. Allaying her fears, answering her doubts. He'd dried her tears and made her laugh. He'd turned this into the most special day of her life.

What he'd said about how they'd each searched for someone to love was true. Jamie had wanted to be married for so many years. She'd hungered for that special relationship and all that went with it, only to be disappointed time after time.

Their dinner check arrived, and while Rich dealt with that, Jamie finished her wine. As she raised the glass to her lips, her gaze fell on the diamond ring on her left hand. It was a simple design, a small diamond set in the center of an antique gold rose. When Rich had first mentioned it, she hadn't felt right about wearing it, but the fit was perfect, and now that it was on her finger she wished she didn't have to take it off.

"I suppose I should drive you home."

Jamie's heart soared at the reluctance she heard in his voice. She wasn't any more eager for this day to end than he was.

"I suppose," she said with an equal lack of enthusiasm.

"You have to work tomorrow?"

Jamie nodded. "You?"

He nodded, too.

They stood, and Rich helped her on with her coat. His hands lingered on her shoulders, and he drew her back against him and breathed in deeply. "Thank you."

"For what?" Jamie twisted around, and the restaurant noises that surrounded them—the laughter and conversation, the clinking of silverware on china—seemed to fade away.

"For marrying me," he whispered. "For agreeing to bear my child."

Jamie pulled the straight skirt over her hips and clipped it to the hanger. She hung it in her closet along with the jacket, then wandered into the kitchen as the teakettle whistled.

Sitting at the table in her full-length slip, she propped her nylon-covered feet on the opposite chair and cradled the mug of hot tea in both hands.

"I'm married," she said aloud, testing the words.

They came back sounding hollow, as hollow as she felt. She hadn't wanted Rich to leave—not so soon. It was barely ten. But when she'd offered him an excuse to stay, he'd turned her down.

So this was her wedding night. In her dreams she'd created a magical fantasy of champagne and romance. See-through nighties and wild, abandoned passion. If this was a traditional marriage, she'd have all that. Instead, she'd chosen something else. Something far less.

She should be happy. Excited. In love.

She *was* all those things—in a manner of speaking. Then why, she asked herself, did the aching loneliness weigh so heavily on her heart?

Rich bent the thick goose-down pillow in half and bunched it beneath his head. Rolling over, he glanced at the clock radio and sighed.

Nearly one. The alarm was set for five-thirty and he had yet to fall asleep.

It wasn't every day a man got married, he reminded himself. It wasn't every man who spent his wedding night alone, either.

Rich had dropped Jamie off at her condo, and although she'd suggested he come in for coffee, he'd refused. He didn't even know why he'd turned her down. Coffee had sounded good.

"Be honest," Rich said aloud. It wasn't the coffee that had enticed him, it was Jamie. She wasn't the most beautiful woman he'd ever met. But she was lovely. It seemed impossible to him that he'd missed it all these years. Was he blind?

He'd had beautiful. Pamela was beauty-queen gorgeous—and so empty inside, so lacking in values and morals, that he had to wonder what had attracted him in the first place. She'd appealed to his vanity, no doubt.

Rich rolled onto his back, tucked his hands beneath his head and stared up at the dark ceiling. It hadn't felt right to leave Jamie. With real disappointment, he'd turned around and walked to his parked car. He'd paused halfway down the steps, resisting the urge to rush back and tell her he'd changed his mind, he'd take that coffee, after all.

Instead he'd returned to an apartment that had never seemed emptier and a bed that had never felt so cold.

The phone on Rich's desk rang, and he automatically reached for it. "Engineering." He didn't take his eyes from the drawings he was reviewing.

"Hi," came the soft feminine reply.

Rich straightened. "Jamie? You're back from the doctor's already?" He checked his watch and was surprised to discover it was nearly four.

"I just got back."

"And?" He couldn't keep the eagerness out of his voice. They'd already had one appointment to see Dr. Fullerton. Rich had gone in with Jamie for the initial visit. They'd sat next to each other in Dr. Fullerton's private office and held hands while the gynecologist explained the procedure in detail.

"And," Jamie said quietly, confidently, "we're going to try for this month."

"This month," Rich repeated. "In case you didn't know, I've always been fond of March. March is one of my favorite months."

"Don't get too excited. It…it might not take, it generally doesn't with the first try."

"April, then. April's a good month. Another one of my all-time favorites."

"It could easily be three or four months," Jamie said with a laugh.

"June, July, August. Who can argue with summer?" Rich found himself smiling, too. He was calculating what month the baby would be due if Jamie got pregnant in March.

"December," she said, apparently interpreting his silence. "How would you feel about a December baby?"

"Jubilant. How about you?"

"It could be January or February." She sounded hesitant, as though she was afraid to put too much stock in everything going so smoothly.

"It'll happen when it happens."

"That was profound!" she said. "The doctor gave me a chart. Every morning, I'm supposed to take my temperature. It'll be slightly elevated when I ovulate. As soon as that happens, I'm to contact his office."

"I'm going with you."

"Rich, that really isn't necessary. It's very sweet of you, but—"

"I thought you knew better than to argue with me."

"I should," she said with mock exasperation. "We've been married nearly a month and I don't think I've won a single argument."

"No wonder married life agrees with me." He kept his voice low, wanting to be sure no one in the vicinity could overhear him. Only Jason knew he was married and he wanted to keep it that way as long as possible. "Call me in the morning," he said.

"Why?"

"Because," he said, leaning back in his chair, "I want to keep my own chart."

The following morning, Rich was in the shower when his phone rang. He turned off the faucet, grabbed a towel and raced across the bedroom.

"Hello!" he yelled into the receiver.

"Ninety-eight point six."

He pulled open the drawer on his nightstand and searched blindly for a pen. Water was raining down from his hair, dripping onto the bed. "Got it."

"Talk to you later."

"Great."

Wednesday morning, Rich waited in bed until he heard from her.

"Ninety-eight point six." She sounded discouraged.

"Hey, nothing says it has to happen right away."

"I keep trying to visualize it."

"What is this? Think yourself pregnant?"

She laughed. "Something like that."

"Call me tomorrow." He reached for his chart and made the notation.

"I will."

Thursday showed no difference, but Friday, Rich knew from the tone of her voice that something was up, and he hoped it was her temperature.

"Ninety-eight point seven…I think. Darn, these thermometers are hard to read. But it's definitely higher."

Rich could envision her sitting on the edge of her bed, squinting, trying to read the tiny lines that marked the thermometer. He made a mental note to buy her a digital one.

"Call Dr. Fullerton."

"Rich, I'm not even sure it's elevated. It could be wishful thinking on my part."

"Call him anyway."

"If you insist."

"I do." He hung up the phone and headed toward the shower, whistling.

It wasn't until later that afternoon that the idea of taking her out to dinner occurred to him. Although they'd been married a month, they didn't see each other often. It had been a conscious decision on Rich's part following their wedding day. In light of how he'd felt when he kissed her, it seemed the safest thing to do. He'd taken her to a movie the weekend after their wedding, and they'd both been ill at ease. Foolish as it seemed, it was almost as if they were afraid of each other. Not once during the entire movie had they touched. Jamie didn't invite him in for coffee afterward. Even now he wasn't sure what he would've done had she offered.

Still, they talked every day. Only last weekend he'd changed the oil in her car while she sewed a couple of loose buttons on his shirts. It was a fair exchange and afterward they'd gone out for hamburgers. Nothing fancy. The tension between them didn't seem to be as great as when they'd gone to the movie.

It was time to try again. There could well be a reason to celebrate, and a night on the town appealed to him. Someplace special. It wasn't every day his wife's temperature was elevated by one tenth of one percent.

Jamie was on her lunch break, and Rich didn't leave a message. He'd call her later.

When he did, she was tied up with a customer. The next time he tried, the bank was closed, so he left a message for her at home.

"This is Prince Charming requesting your presence for dinner. Don't eat until you talk to me. I'm on my way home now. Call me there."

Rich expected a message from Jamie to be waiting for him when he arrived at his apartment. There wasn't.

He tried her again at six, six-fifteen, six-thirty and six-forty-five, leaving a message all four times.

By seven o'clock, he was worried. A thousand possibilities crowded his mind, none of them pleasant. He paced the living room in an effort to convince himself he was overreacting, then dialed her number one last time. He listened to her recording yet again, and seethed anxiously during the long beep.

"Jamie, where the hell are you?" he demanded.

Six

Jamie checked her watch, keeping her wrist below the table, hoping she wasn't being obvious. Eight-thirty! She'd been trapped listening to the endless details of Floyd Bacon's divorce for three solid hours.

"Don't you agree?" he asked, looking over at her.

She nodded, although she had no idea what she was agreeing to. A yawn came and she attempted to swallow it, didn't succeed and tactfully pressed her fingers to her lips. Floyd was such a nice man and she was trying hard to disguise her boredom.

"My goodness, look at the time," Floyd said.

It had all started so innocently.

Jamie had dated Floyd about five years ago. He was a regular customer at the bank and they'd seen each other off and on for a six-month period. Nothing serious, nothing even close to serious. Then he'd met Carolyn and the two of them had fallen in love and married. Jamie had attended their wedding. She remembered what she bought them for a wedding gift—a set of stainless steel flatware with rosebuds on the handles. He and Carolyn had bought a house a few months later. Jamie had handled the loan application for them, but when they'd moved, they'd switched their account to a branch closer to where they lived. In the past three years, Carolyn had quit work to stay home with their two young children.

"I can't tell you how sorry I am the marriage didn't work out," Jamie said, wondering what could possibly have gone wrong between two people who so obviously loved each other. She would never have suspected this would happen to Floyd and Carolyn, of all people. Of all *couples*.

"I'm sorry, too," Floyd said. His dark eyes touched her with their sadness. He'd moved into an apartment and had stopped at the bank to open a checking account. But a new account was only a pretext, Jamie soon learned; for airing his frustration with Carolyn, his marriage, his two preschool children and life in general.

Floyd had arrived just before closing time, lingered until he was the last customer in the bank and then asked Jamie to join him for a drink. She'd hesitated, but he'd looked so downtrodden and miserable that she'd gone against her better judgment. A drink soon turned into two and then Floyd suggested they have something to eat. At the time, it had seemed reasonable, but that was an hour and a half ago.

"I really should be going home," she said, reaching for her purse. It was Friday night and the workweek had seemed extra-long and she was tired. Keeping track of her temperature and charting it was draining her emotional energy.

No, she decided, talking to Rich every morning was responsible for that. Speaking to him first thing, discussing the intimate details of her reproductive system, hearing his enthusiasm...talking about their child. Nothing had prepared her for the effect all this was having. She lived for those brief two-minute calls. It was almost as if he were in bed beside her...almost as if he were holding her in his arms. This closeness she felt toward him frightened her. The magnitude of what they'd done, of what they were planning, the child they'd conceive together, had brought subtle and not-so-subtle changes to their relationship.

Earlier in the day she'd hoped and planned to have a relaxing Friday night—to soak in a hot bath and cuddle up in bed with a good book. She might have given Rich a call and invited him over for dinner. There was a new recipe she wanted to try and he seemed to enjoy her home-cooked meals. She'd only seen him twice in the past month, and it didn't seem enough.

"I'll follow you home," Floyd said, breaking into her thoughts. He tossed some money on the table for the waitress.

It would be too late to call Rich now. Tomorrow was her Saturday morning to work, but she could call him then and ask him over for dinner on either Saturday or Sunday. Friday nights were probably busy for him, so it wasn't likely he would've been home anyway.

"Jamie?"

"I'm sorry. My mind was a million miles away. There's no need for you to see me home, Floyd."

"I know, but I'd feel better if I knew you got there safely."

She nodded. Floyd really was a nice man, and she did feel sorry for him. If lending an ear had helped him, she shouldn't complain. The time would come soon enough when she'd need a shoulder to cry on herself. Once the baby was born, she'd be filing for divorce. The thought was a cheerless one.

Jamie lived less than fifteen minutes from the bank and it was on Floyd's way to his new apartment, so she didn't object strongly when he insisted on following her.

When she pulled into her assigned parking space, he waited until she was out of her car. She waved to let him know she was safe and sound.

Floyd lowered his car window and said, "I appreciate being able to talk to you, Jamie. You're a good friend to both Carolyn and me."

"I'm happy if I was any help."

The sadness returned to Floyd's eyes. "I really love her, you know."

Jamie nodded. She believed him. Divorce was usually so ugly and there was so much pain involved. Jamie had seen several of her friends traumatized by the breakup of their marriages.

"Are you sure you really want this divorce?" she asked impulsively. Surely if two people deeply loved each other, they could work something out, couldn't they?

He shook his head. "I never did want a divorce. Carolyn's the one who…well, you know." His shoulders rose in a deep sigh.

"You're sure about that?"

Floyd hesitated. "I'm pretty sure. When I told her I was moving out, she didn't say a word to stop me. The way I figure it, if she really loved me, she would've asked me to stay."

"What if she assumed that if you really loved her, you'd never *want* to move?"

Floyd stared at her. "You think that's what she might've thought?"

"I don't know, but it's worth asking, don't you think?"

"Yeah…I do," Floyd said, his voice revealing the first enthusiasm she'd heard all evening. He raised his car window, then quickly lowered it again. "Jamie?"

"Yes?" She was halfway toward the outside stairs that led to her second-floor condominium.

"Would you mind if I used your phone? My cell's dead, and I'd like to give Carolyn a call to see if she wants to talk."

"Sure." Smiling, she opened her purse and took out her key. If she'd mentioned this earlier she thought wryly, she might've been home two hours ago.

Floyd parked his car, then hurried up the stairs with her. He resembled a young boy, he was so eager. She unlocked the door and flipped on the light switch. Floyd immediately headed for her phone.

Jamie made herself scarce for a couple of minutes, going into her bedroom to remove her shoes. She hung up her jacket and eased her gray blouse from her waistband. Before leaving her bedroom, she slipped her feet into her fuzzy open-toed slippers. Then she went into the kitchen and put the kettle on the burner. As soon as Floyd was gone, she planned to relax with a cup of herbal tea.

"Carolyn agrees we should talk," Floyd announced triumphantly as he replaced the telephone receiver. "She sounded pleased to hear from me. Do you think she's lonely? I doubt it," he answered his own question before Jamie had a chance. "Carolyn always did have lots of friends, and she isn't one to sit home and cry in her soup, if you know what I mean."

Jamie nodded. "I hope this works out for you."

"Me, too. I'll be heading out now," Floyd said. "She's getting a sitter for the kids and she's going to meet me for a cup of coffee."

The doorbell chimed then, in long impatient bursts. Floyd's gaze swung to Jamie. She couldn't imagine who'd be arriving this late.

She walked past Floyd and opened her door. No sooner had she turned the lock than Rich raced in as though he was there to put out a fire.

"Where the hell have you been?" he demanded. "I've been half out of my—" He stopped midstep and midsentence when he caught sight of Floyd and the color drained from his face. His eyes widened with shock, disbelief and…could it be pain? Slowly he turned toward Jamie.

"Floyd, this is Rich Manning," she said, gesturing from one to the other. "Rich, Floyd Bacon."

Floyd held out his hand, and for a moment, Jamie feared Rich wasn't going to take it. He did so, but with ill grace. "I take it Jamie didn't mention me," he said sarcastically.

"Ah…no," Floyd said, rubbing his palms together. He eyed the front door. "Listen, I was just leaving."

"No need to rush," Rich said, sitting down on the sofa and crossing his long legs. He stretched his arm against the back of the cushions, giving the impression that he had plenty of time to sit and chat. "I'm interested in hearing how the two of you spent the evening." His smile lacked warmth or welcome.

"Rich," Jamie said, stepping forward. She'd never seen him like this, so sarcastic and ill-mannered.

One look from him cut her to the quick. Rarely had anyone looked at her with such… disdain. He studied her, from her slippers to the blouse she'd pulled free from her skirt, and his eyes narrowed, damning her.

"Jamie's an old friend," Floyd explained. "I was in the bank this afternoon and…well, you see, my wife and I have separated, and Jamie—"

"So you're married, *too*."

"Too?" Frowning, Floyd turned to Jamie for an explanation.

"Yes," Rich said in a deceptively calm voice. "Jamie and I've been married…what is it now, darling, a month?"

"Rich," she warned him under her breath. He might be her legal husband, a man she'd known and respected for more than a decade, but seeing him behave like this, talk like this, he seemed like a total stranger.

"Jamie. My goodness," Floyd said, sounding astonished. "You didn't say a word about being married. Congratulations! I wish you'd said something earlier."

"So do I," Rich added caustically.

Once again Floyd glanced at the door. "I'd like to stay and chat, but I really should leave. My wife and I are going to meet and talk... Jamie was the one who suggested it. Well, actually, I came up with the idea of calling Carolyn, but Jamie helped me see that it was the right thing to do." He spoke rapidly, the words coming out so fast they tumbled over one another. "I'll see you later."

Jamie held the door for him. "Thanks for dinner," she said as graciously as the circumstances allowed.

"Thanks for dinner," Rich mimicked derisively as Floyd went out the door.

Jamie felt a storm threatening. One of anger and frustration. The thundercloud was sitting directly behind her, and she did her best to restrain her indignation. After taking a moment to compose herself, she turned around. "Is something bothering you, Rich?" she asked in a level voice.

He leapt off the sofa as though he'd been sitting on a giant spring. "Is something *bothering* me?" he repeated coldly. "What do you think you're doing, dating that joker?"

"It wasn't a date."

"I heard you thank him for dinner." He spat out the words as though to have to say them was a detestable task. "At least you could've returned my phone calls."

"I...haven't checked my messages. Good grief, I didn't get home until five minutes ago." Moving across the room, she went to her phone to listen. Six messages, all from Rich, played back, each sounding progressively less patient and increasingly anxious. The last one had been to demand to know "where the hell" she was.

"When I couldn't stand waiting for you to call, I drove over here to wait for you. Lo and behold, your car was in your parking space and you were here—with *Floyd*."

"I can understand your concern," Jamie said calmly, willing to grant him that much.

"You're my wife, dammit! How am I supposed to feel when you turn up missing?" He raked his fingers through his hair and stalked to the opposite side of the room.

Jamie drew in a long, soothing breath, determined not to let this escalate into a full-fledged argument. "I was never missing. I'm sorry I worried you, Rich, but you're overreacting, and frankly, it's beginning to annoy me."

"Annoy *you?* I've been pacing the floor for the past three hours...."

"I would have phoned."

"You brought a man home with you!" He made it sound as though that was grounds for divorce.

"Floyd's an old friend."

The kettle whistled, and Jamie hurried into the kitchen and turned off the burner, all thought of tea forgotten. The boiling water bubbled from the spout, nearly scalding her. Rich had followed, stalking into the room behind her.

"Apparently you don't have a problem letting *old friends* take you out to dinner," he accused her, his words inflamed with impatience.

Jamie gritted her teeth, biting back an angry retort. "He needed someone to talk to, someone who'd listen to his problems. You're making it sound as though I did something underhanded. I was just being a friend."

"You're a married woman," Rich bellowed. He slammed his fist on the counter. "*My* wife. How do you think it makes me feel, knowing you chose to go out to dinner with another man instead of your own husband?"

"I didn't choose Floyd over you! Good heavens, how was I supposed to know you wanted to take me to dinner? I'm not a mind reader."

"If you'd come home after work the way you're supposed to, you would have heard the first of my six messages."

"That's ridiculous! I can't run my life according to your whims." She'd managed to keep her temper intact, but she didn't know how much longer her precarious hold would last.

"I thought you were different." A spark of pain flashed in his eyes.

"What do you mean by *that?*"

"I would've trusted you with my life, but you're like every other woman I've ever known. The minute my back's turned, you think nothing of seeing someone else."

The emptiness in his voice cut at Jamie's heart. "That's so unfair."

"We're married, and even that didn't make a difference." His eyes accused her of—what? Being unfaithful? That was completely irrational!

"This isn't a real marriage and you know it," she said heatedly. Her voice was shaking with the effort to keep from shouting. "You're the one who insisted on the ceremony, but it was for convenience."

"We're married!"

"Maybe, but you have no right to storm into my home and insult my guests."

"And *you* have no right to bring a man home with you."

"That's ridiculous." Jamie couldn't believe they were having this conversation. "Our marriage is in name only for…for obvious reasons."

"We said our vows."

"Don't remind me." The promises they'd made to each other continued to haunt her.

"Clearly someone has to."

"Oh-h-h," Jamie seethed. Tightening her fists at her sides, she exhaled sharply and resisted the urge to bang her cupboard doors to vent her frustration.

"Temper, temper."

"I think you'd better leave before we say something we'll regret." Instinct had told her that getting married wouldn't work, and she'd ignored it. Now she was suffering the consequences.

"Not on your life."

"This is my home," Jamie cried, quickly losing her grip on her rage. She'd never known Rich could be so unreasonable, so rude, so… impossible.

"You're just like every other woman I've ever known," Rich repeated in unflattering tones.

"And you're just like every other man, so wrapped up in your own ego that it'd take a whack on the head with a two-by-four to see what's right in front of your nose."

"It wasn't *me* who went out behind *your* back," he shouted. He leaned against the kitchen counter and crossed his arms.

"Why do you care if I had dinner with a dozen men?" she demanded. "It never bothered you before!"

"We weren't married before."

"I'm not your possession," she said. "You have no right, husband or not, to tell me who I can see and who I can't."

"The hell I don't."

Jamie squeezed her eyes shut. "I *knew* this wasn't going to work… I told you it wouldn't, but would you listen? Oh, no, you knew so much better."

"I still do."

Jamie couldn't help it, she stamped her foot. She hadn't done anything so childish since junior high. "Look at us," she cried, her voice shaking with anger. "I'm…I'm not even pregnant yet and already we're fighting. We're going to ruin everything fighting over something so…stupid."

"It isn't stupid to me."

"Floyd is just a friend. For heaven's sake, he's married!"

"So are you."

"Why are you doing this?" she cried.

"All I'm asking is that you keep your part of the bargain and I'll keep mine. That shouldn't be so difficult."

"Oh, right," she said, walking around the table and leaning on the back of a chair. "There's a lot more involved in this arrangement than I ever knew about or agreed to and—"

"Like what?"

"Like…like your caveman attitude toward me."

"Caveman? Because I don't want my wife dating another man—another *married* man?" He glared across the room at her. "Forgive me if I'm wrong, but I seem to remember a phrase or two in the wedding vows that state—"

"Don't you dare." Jamie pointed an accusing finger at his chest. "Don't you *dare,*" she repeated. "I never wanted to go through with the wedding, and you knew it. Using it against me now is the height of unfairness."

"We're married, Jamie, whether you like it or not."

"I don't like it, I hate it. I hate everything about it—this is the biggest mistake of my life." Unable to bear any more arguing, she whirled around and covered her face with her hands. If there was any decency left in him, Rich Manning would go. He'd leave her alone.

Jamie's nerves were raw, and the hair at the nape of her neck bristled as she heard Rich walk toward her. The clipped pace of his steps did nothing to reassure her.

"Did he kiss you?"

"No!" she shouted, furious that he'd ask such an outrageous question.

"Good, because I'm going to." His hands moved over her shoulders, clasping them, holding her in place.

"No." She made one weak protest, but she didn't know who she was talking to, Rich or herself. He'd kissed her once, the day of their wedding, and it had obsessed her ever since. She couldn't allow him to destroy her equilibrium again, destroy her peace of mind.

Although she resisted, Rich turned her around to face him. Jamie was on fire, and he'd barely touched her.

Rich took hold of her chin, his fingers firm,

yet oddly gentle. Without another word, he bent down and covered her mouth with his own. Jamie knew she shouldn't let him do this. Not in the heat of anger. Not when they were fighting. Not when his kiss would only create a need for more.

He tasted so good, so wonderful. It wasn't *fair*. Nothing about this so-called marriage was fair.

He moved his mouth over hers, shaping her lips with his own until she moaned. It seemed to be what he was waiting for. The instant her lips parted, his tongue swept inside.

Shock waves vibrated through her at the small, ruthless movements of his tongue. Jamie could feel herself melting against him. The need continued to build within her, licking at her senses, growing hotter and stronger and fiercer....

Not satisfied with her lips alone, he kissed her eyes, her throat, until Jamie felt as if she was about to ignite.

A frightening excitement exploded inside her, going beyond mere pleasure and quickly advancing to a demand so intense there would be no turning back for either of them.

"Rich...no." She braced her hands against

his chest, wanting to use that leverage to break away.

"Yes," he countered with a groan. His arms circled her waist, and he lifted her effortlessly from the floor, adjusting her hips against his own so she was aware of what she was doing to him—of the need she'd created in him.

Jamie slipped her arms around his neck, inclined her head and kissed him back. She felt sensual, wanton... and a little scared.

A low, rough sound rumbled from deep within his throat.

"Rich...please, oh, please, we've got to stop." Her heart was reeling with excitement but she was terrified of where this might lead. Terrified that, after tonight, she'd never be able to live with a marriage that wasn't a marriage.

"Not yet." He pressed his lips to her neck, running the tip of his tongue across the smooth skin of her throat and up the underside of her jaw. Jamie threw back her head. A ribbon of warm pleasure braided its way down her spine.

She buried her fingers in his hair and sighed, feeling breathless and hot. So breathless she could barely gulp in enough air. So hot. Hotter than she'd ever been.

He lifted her higher, leaning her against the kitchen counter. His hands worked the buttons of her blouse, sliding it from her shoulders. Her bra closed in the back, and he reached for and found the clasp.

"Tell me what you want," he whispered, caressing her thighs, stroking them as he spread delicate, moist kisses across her neck.

"I...don't know."

"Funny, I do," he countered with a lazy, sexy laugh. "You want me."

Jamie couldn't disagree. She could barely speak as a powerful coil of need tightened within her.

"Deny it." His tongue moistened a trail from the hollow at the base of her throat to her trembling chin.

"I can't."

"Me, neither." He swept her from the counter, shifting her weight until she was completely in his arms. He carried her as if she weighed nothing at all and headed out of the kitchen. He paused to turn off the light.

"Rich." She had to say something before it was too late. "We'll regret this in the morning." Even as she spoke, she wound her arms around his neck.

"Maybe." He didn't bother to deny it, but it didn't stop him, either.

Her bedroom was dark. Moonlight splashed

through the open drapes, and Rich slowly lowered her onto the bed.

There was no turning back now.

Seven

They were silent afterward, their breathing labored, their chests heaving. Rich wished Jamie would say something. Anything. She didn't, and slowly reality returned, inexplicably linked with the glory of what they'd shared.

Rich kissed her softly, gently, with none of the urgency he'd felt earlier. He slid his fingers into the silky length of her hair and sighed with satisfaction. He kissed her again, reveling in her warm, sweet taste. He longed for her to tell him she experienced no remorse over their lovemaking. He'd been so angry, such a jealous idiot, and one thing had led to another. Before he could stop it, they were making love. She'd warned him, claimed they'd be left with regrets, but he felt none. Only a powerful sense of honesty.

Rich realized his weight was too much for her, but when he tried to move, she resisted, tightening her hold on him, hooking her ankles over his.

"Don't leave me," she whispered.

"No." He had no intention of doing so. "But I'm too heavy for you."

"Stay with me like this. Please." She stroked his back, her touch featherlight.

He would stay like this because she asked, but only for a little while. They both needed sleep and the thought of waking up beside her thrilled him almost as much as the memory of everything they'd done together in the last hour.

The silvery moonlight illuminated her face. He noticed that her eyes were languorous, her face flushed with pleasure. Her lips were turned up slightly in a secret smile. A serene, womanly smile. Just watching her, *loving* her, brought him peace. Because he did love her, and he was astonished that he hadn't recognized it earlier. Astonished at his own lack of perception. The love he felt for her burned within his chest, literally burned. The depth of emotion he felt had everything to do with this woman, and the profound pleasure he'd experienced was only part of that.

Her skin felt like silk beneath his hands as he brushed his fingertips down the side of her face. She sighed, and her breath caught in her throat.

Rarely had Rich experienced such contentment. The magnitude of it left him feeling weak and humble. Tucking his arms securely around Jamie's waist, he rolled onto his back, taking her with him. She made a small sound of surprise, then smiled peacefully, nestled her head on his chest and closed her eyes. Within minutes, she was asleep.

Slumber didn't claim him as quickly. He remained in awe of the emotions crowding his heart. For years he'd been blind and deaf when it came to his feelings for Jamie. Others had seen it. James had immediately recognized the love Rich felt for her and said as much. Rich had been quick to laugh and deny what was obvious to everyone but himself.

It had taken an argument to push him over the edge, push them both past the point of no return. If he had any regrets, it was that this discovery had come so late—and on the heels of a heated exchange.

He sighed and watched Jamie in the moonlight. She slept, utterly tranquil, and his heart swelled with a love so strong it was all he could do not to wake her and tell her what he was feeling. He wanted to, but it would be selfish not to let her sleep. He kissed her temple and closed his eyes, content to keep his wife secure in his arms.

Sometime toward dawn, Rich woke. Jamie was sleeping on her side and he was cuddling her, their bodies pressed intimately together. He smiled, a smile that came from his heart. They were like a long-married couple, completely comfortable with each other, as though they'd been sleeping together for years.

This was exactly what Rich intended, to continue sleeping with Jamie night after night for the rest of their lives. They'd grow old that way, gracefully, together. God willing, they'd raise several children, who'd be sheltered by the love their parents shared.

Rich stirred once more a little after six. Yawning, he stretched his arms above his head. He'd been working a lot of extra hours on a contract Boeing had with the government and he needed to get to work soon, despite the weekend.

He slipped out of bed and gazed down on Jamie, then leaned over and gently kissed her forehead. Hurrying to the shower, he whistled a cheerful tune.

In a joyous mood, Rich sang at the top of his lungs. He expected Jamie to be awake when he returned to the bedroom, but was disappointed to discover she was still asleep. He dressed and went out the door. He'd phone her later, as soon as he had a chance. He tended to get involved in his work and forget about the time, but he'd try not to let that happen. They had to talk.

Jamie woke at eight. Although she was sleeping on her side, facing the wall, she sensed almost immediately that Rich had gone.

He'd left without a word. Abandoned her to deal with the emptiness of the morning. Alone.

Closing her eyes, she bit her lower lip. The feeling of betrayal, of total isolation, was unlike anything she'd ever experienced.

Their argument played back in her mind, over and over. Every ugly word they'd said, the accusations, the hurt, echoed in her mind, taunting her again and again.

His reaction the night before made perfect sense in the bright light of morning. It must've been more than his pride could take to find her with Floyd. Something inside Rich had cracked.

Her evening with Floyd, no matter how innocent, must've been like a slap in Rich's face. He'd reacted in anger and pain, not because he cared. The reason for his outburst was directly related to his male ego. What had started out as an argument had eventually progressed to a physical exchange.

Rich had kissed her. First in anger. Then in need. A need fed by frustration and jealousy. He might not want a real marriage, but his pride demanded at least the pretense.

The image of her husband standing in her kitchen was unforgettable. He'd been furious with her. Although she'd had her back to him at the time, she knew she'd outraged him when she'd said that their marriage was the biggest mistake of her life.

A terrible tension had followed, so impenetrable that Jamie doubted she could've said or done anything to relieve it. Sitting up in bed, she pushed her tangled hair away from her face.

Rich hadn't kissed her for any of the right reasons. He'd done it because he hadn't believed her. He assumed Floyd had kissed her, and he couldn't tolerate another woman cheating on him—even if it was only in his imagination.

During all the years of their friendship,

Jamie had seen Rich as distinct from the other men she'd known. That had been the first of several mistakes. Rich was exactly like them, competitive and territorial.

A few weeks earlier, he'd attempted to set her up with his engineering friend, Bill whatever-his-name-was. Now Rich couldn't stand her speaking to another man, even someone as blameless as Floyd Bacon. Good grief, Floyd was married! Did Rich honestly think she'd stoop to that level? Apparently he did, which didn't say much for his opinion of her.

She'd never seen Rich act more irrational. He'd refused to listen to her explanation, had been rude and arrogant in the extreme. And for what reason? None! At least none she could understand.

What he'd said about their being married was true enough—on paper. But their relationship wasn't any different now than it had been before the ceremony.

Except that it was. Everything she'd feared was coming to pass.

They'd been married a month, and look what had happened. It wouldn't depress her quite as much if Rich hadn't left her to face the morning alone. The questions tormented her, eroding her pride and self-confidence.

If only he'd said something afterward.

If only she'd said something.

It had all been so beautiful. Their lovemaking had captured her heart, her soul.

Jamie had longed to tell him everything she was feeling, but she'd been afraid. Afraid he hadn't experienced the same wonder. Afraid he'd be embarrassed. Afraid he had regrets. She couldn't have borne knowing that, not when everything had been so perfect for her.

Evidently he'd had second thoughts, otherwise he wouldn't have abandoned her, slipping away like a thief in the night.

Reluctantly, Jamie climbed out of bed and into the shower. The pulsating spray struck her skin like dull needles. The need to release her anguish in the form of tears left her throat aching and raw, but she refused to cry. She didn't have the time. It was her turn to work the Saturday morning shift at the bank. She was already behind schedule.

Wrapping a towel around herself, she went back into her bedroom—and came to a sudden stop. She covered her cheeks with her hands, mortified to find her carelessly discarded clothes from one end of the room to the other. The memory of how eager they'd been for each other added to her shame and humiliation.

Jamie dressed quickly, then hung last night's clothes in the farthest reaches of her closet and hurried out the door, not bothering with more than a cup of instant coffee.

Rich tried phoning Jamie at quarter to ten. Surely she'd be up and about by then. The phone rang three times before he was invited to "leave a message." He hung up. Later, he promised himself. He'd try later.

It was noon before he had a chance to call again. When she still didn't answer, he became irritated and set the receiver down harder than he'd intended.

"Problems?" Bill Hastings asked, walking into Rich's office.

"Not really." He did his best to appear nonchalant.

"Don't try to kid me," Bill said, sitting on the corner of Rich's desk, his left foot dangling. "I know the look when I see it—I've worn it often enough myself. You've got woman problems."

It wouldn't do any good to deny it, so he said nothing.

"Pamela?"

"Not this time."

Bill's eyebrows shot upward. "Someone else? You've been lying low lately. I didn't know you were seeing anyone."

"I'm not...exactly." It was a half-truth, which also made it a half lie. He *wasn't* seeing anyone. He was a married man, only Bill didn't know that and Rich wasn't in any mood to announce it now. Not when he didn't know what was going on between him and Jamie.

Last night had been good for them. Every time he remembered their lovemaking, his head spun and he felt warm inside. It wasn't a sensation he was familiar with, since he'd never experienced anything like it in other relationships.

He'd thought, at least he'd hoped, that Jamie had shared in the magic they'd created, but apparently that wasn't the case.

At two, Rich decided to try Jamie one last time. He might be reading more into her not answering the phone than she intended. Maybe she simply wasn't there to answer it. After all, Saturdays were often busy with errands.

He'd phone again and if there still wasn't any answer, the hell with it. A man had his pride.

He'd wait until she called him.

* * *

The phone was ringing when Jamie, struggling with a bag of groceries, tried to remove the key from her purse and unlock her front door. Once she'd thrown open the door she raced across the room, praying with everything in her that it was Rich.

"Hello," she cried breathlessly after making a leap for the phone. Whoever it was had apparently just hung up, and a buzz droned in her ear.

She knew the caller couldn't have been Rich. He'd left six messages the night before. He wouldn't be shy about leaving another.

On the off chance he had, she listened impatiently through all the messages she hadn't yet erased.

Nothing new from Rich. Nothing.

The emptiness around her seemed to swell. Her heart felt like a lead weight in her chest as she walked across her living room and closed the door. She'd dropped her bag of groceries on the sofa as she dashed for the phone. The apples had tumbled out, along with a box of cold cereal and a bottle of imported wine.

Like a romantic fool, she'd gone and purchased an expensive bottle of wine. Her morning had been hectic—Saturdays at the bank generally were. But no matter how many customers she served, or how many loan applications she reviewed, Jamie hadn't been able to stop thinking about Rich.

She'd been wrong—he *wasn't* like other men she'd known. She'd loved him too long to condemn him on such flimsy evidence. There were any number of reasons he might've had to leave. She was a sound sleeper, and for all she knew, he could've tried to wake her. By the time she'd left the bank at a little after one, Jamie was confident she'd hear from Rich. Confident enough to rush out and buy a bottle of wine and a small sirloin tip roast just so she could invite him over to dinner—so they could talk.

There was a lot to say.

Rich stared at the phone accusingly, willing it to ring. He'd arrived home late Saturday afternoon. He was in such a rush to listen to his messages that he didn't even stop to check his mail. He bounded up the stairs to his apartment, taking two and three steps at a time, sure there'd be some word from Jamie.

The blinking red message light made him feel almost cocky with relief. Until he discov-

ered it was Jason who'd phoned. Jason, not
Jamie. His brother, not his wife.

So this was what it meant to be married, to
wear his heart on his sleeve and mope around
like a besotted fool. So this was how it felt to
truly love another person. To care so much that
his whole life hinged on a single phone call.

Rich was through with waiting. He'd already ruined one night pacing the floors like
a madman, yearning to hear from Jamie. He'd
be damned before he'd do it again anytime
soon.

Furthermore, he mused darkly, he was
through with allowing a woman to rule his
heart. Apparently he hadn't learned his les-
son, after all.

Pamela had strung him along for weeks.
He'd been duped by one woman and he wasn't
going through *that* again.

If Jamie was foolish enough to throw away
the best thing that had ever happened to either of them, then so be it. The choice rested
entirely with her and he wasn't going to say a
word to persuade her. Not a single word.

Clearly she felt none of the beauty of their
night together. None of the wonder and the
magic. It stung his pride that he could have
misread her so completely.

Rather than dwell on his marriage, Rich reached for the phone and viciously punched out his older brother's number. Jason answered on the second ring, and they made plans for the evening. Nothing fancy. Paul, their oldest brother, had invited them over for a round-robin of pinochle. A card game sounded a lot more inviting than sitting home all night waiting for a silent phone to ring.

Call him. Jamie had never spent a more restless Saturday afternoon and evening in her life. Pride, she soon discovered, made poor company.

For all she knew, he could be just as eagerly waiting for her to call him. But that didn't make sense, especially since he'd been the one to slip away in the early morning hours. Even so, she was willing to give him the benefit of the doubt. *More* than willing.

Although her stomach was in knots, she'd gone about cooking an elaborate dinner, just in case Rich did phone. The roast and small red potatoes gave her a perfect excuse to invite him over. Now the meal sat on her stove untouched. Unappreciated. Forsaken. Just like her.

When she could bear the silence no longer,

Jamie walked over to the phone. Her hand was trembling and she paused to clear her throat twice while she was dialing. She forced herself to smile, determined to sound as cheerful as a robin in springtime when Rich answered the phone.

Only he didn't.

After four rings, his machine came on.

Jamie was so stunned, she listened for a couple of seconds, then reluctantly hung up. For several moments, her hand remained on the receiver as the futility and the discouragement overwhelmed her.

She was being silly. Naive. But it had never occurred to her, not once, that Rich wouldn't be home.

Apparently he'd gone out for the evening. No doubt he was having fun, laughing it up with his friends, enjoying himself while she sat home alone.

There were places she could go, people to see, fun she could have, too. She contacted three friends and suggested a movie. It was a sad statement on her life that the most exciting entertainment she could think of was a movie.

All three of her friends already had plans for the evening. Which was just as well, since Jamie wasn't all that keen to go out anyway.

It was the kind of night for watching reruns on television with a box of crackers in her lap and a six-pack of diet soda at her side.

Rich had a great time Saturday night. They'd played cards into the early hours of the morning and thoroughly enjoyed themselves. There'd been whole stretches of time when he didn't think of Jamie at all. Five-and ten-minute blocks of time.

Things would've gone well if it hadn't been for Jason. His brother seemed to like walking close to the edge, Rich thought with annoyance.

"So how's the marriage of *in*convenience working out?" Jason had asked on the drive home. He made it sound like a joke, but Rich wasn't in a laughing mood.

Rather than go into any of the details, Rich gave an unintelligible reply.

"What's that?" Jason pressed.

"I didn't say anything."

"I know."

"Just drop it, Jason." Rich was serious and he made sure his brother knew it. He didn't want to discuss his relationship with Jamie. What she'd said the night before about their marriage being the worst mistake of her life was beginning to have the ring of truth to it.

"So," Jason added after a few minutes, "marriage isn't exactly a bed of roses, is it?"

"I never claimed it would be."

"Is she pregnant yet?"

"Pregnant?" Rich repeated the word as though he'd never heard it before. "Pregnant," he said again, his voice dropping. Vividly he recalled their conversation Friday morning and how excited he'd been when he learned her temperature had been slightly elevated. They'd spoken every morning for several days running, discussing the chances of pregnancy. It was the reason they were married! Only, they'd planned to conceive the child by non-traditional means....

Twenty-four hours following his conversation with his brother, Rich continued to mull over the possibility of a pregnancy.

He hadn't heard from Jamie all day Sunday, either. He'd decided he probably wouldn't. That woman was so stubborn. Fine, he'd wait her out. If she didn't contact him, it was her loss.

He changed his mind Monday afternoon. It was either call her or resign from his engineering job. He'd made one mistake after another all day. Every time the phone rang, he felt as though an electrical shock had gone through him and nearly leaped off his chair. Although he strove to sound cool and collected, he couldn't keep his heart from speeding like a race-car engine.

Obviously Rich would have to be the one to call. It felt like blackmail, which did little to improve his mood. He stood and closed the door to his office.

He walked all the way around his desk twice, then sat heavily in his chair and picked up the phone.

The bank's receptionist answered almost immediately.

"Is Jamie…Warren available?" He stopped himself from asking for Jamie Manning just in time.

"I'll transfer your call," the woman said, cutting him off. The phone rang three times, frustrating Rich even more.

"This is Jamie Warren's office. How may I help you?"

"Ah…" Rich had expected Jamie would answer. "Is Jamie available?"

"No, I'm sorry, she's home sick today. May I help you?"

"Ah…" Jamie was home sick? She'd seemed in perfect health Friday night. Perhaps she was ill. Too ill to call him.

"Sir? May I help you?" the woman repeated

"No…no, thanks. I'll phone later."

But first he was going to find out exactly what was wrong with Jamie.

Eight

Jamie felt wretched. Not only had she spent the most miserable weekend of her life, but late Sunday afternoon she'd come down with a ferocious case of the flu.

Monday morning she'd phoned in sick. For most of the day she'd stayed in bed, trying to convince herself that it was a twenty-four-hour virus and she'd be fine by Tuesday morning.

Her head throbbed, her muscles ached and she was sure she had a fever. If she wasn't so sick, she'd get out of bed to take her temperature. The only times she'd risked leaving the comfort of her warm cocoon had been to make trips to the bathroom.

The phone at her bedside rang and she reached for it blindly, nearly toppling a glass of liquid flu medication left from the night before.

"Hello," she croaked. It was probably some salesman hoping to sell her a cemetery plot. The timing couldn't be better.

"Jamie?"

"Rich?" Naturally he'd phone her *now,* when her defenses were down and she was too weak to react. She'd waited three painful days to hear from him. Nightmare days.

Now that he'd called, Jamie experienced absolutely no emotion. Certainly not relief. Or anger, although she'd spent most of Sunday furious with him, and so hurt it was all she could do not to simply give in to self-pity.

"I phoned the bank and they told me you were home sick," he explained, as though he needed a reason to call her.

"I've got the flu."

A slight hesitation followed. "You're sure? Have you been to the doctor?"

"I'm too sick for that." She found his concern laughable. He'd walked out on her. Ignored her. Hurt her. And now he was upset because she hadn't seen a doctor over a twenty-four-hour flu bug?

Once again Rich hesitated. "I think you should make an appointment with Dr. Fullerton."

"Dr. Fullerton?" she echoed. Rich wasn't

making sense. "Why would I see a gynecologist?"

"Because what you have might not be the flu," he returned, his words sounding as though they were spoken from between clenched teeth.

Maybe she was being obtuse, but she didn't understand what he was saying. "Trust me, it's the flu. I've got all the symptoms."

"Didn't it dawn on you that it might be something else?" His voice rose with impatience.

"No. Should it?"

"Yes!"

It hit Jamie like a bolt of lightning. Rich thought she might be pregnant! If it wasn't so ludicrous she'd cry. He actually seemed worried.

"It's too soon to tell," she said in her most formal voice, as if she were relaying the bank's decision regarding a loan application. "But it's unlikely."

"Your temperature was elevated, remember?"

"Not that much. Don't worry, you're safe."

His angry sigh told her that either he was exasperated or furious—Jamie didn't know which.

When would she learn? Time after time she'd foolishly handed her heart to a man, and the outcome was always the same. Within a few months her heart would be broken, shattered, and she'd be limping away. Some women were meant to find love, but apparently she wasn't one of them. Some women were destined to have forty or fifty years of contented marital bliss. She'd be lucky if *her* marriage lasted two months.

"Do you need anything?" Rich asked.

"No." She made her reply as clipped as she could. If he really cared, he wouldn't have left her on Saturday morning. "I'm perfectly fine."

"Then why weren't you at work?"

"Because I've got the flu," she said again.

"Then you aren't *perfectly fine,* are you?"

How like a man to argue about semantics. "Other than the flu, I'm feeling wonderful." She tried to sound as if she'd practically be running the bank single-handed if it weren't for this virus. There certainly wasn't any problem in her life—other than an almost-husband who had no regard for her feelings.

"We need to talk," Rich suggested after an awkward moment. The silence between them was strained—as strained as their marriage.

"I…think that might be a good idea."

"When?"

"Uh…" Jamie stalled for a few seconds. She didn't want to see him anytime soon, considering the pitiful way she was feeling. If she looked remotely as dreadful as she felt, Rich would drag her bodily into Dr. Fullerton's office.

"Wednesday night?" Rich said impatiently.

"Wednesday…sure." By then she should be well on the road to recovery.

"The Cookie Jar?"

The restaurant was one they'd frequented in high school. A little hole-in-the-wall diner with a polished linoleum floor and an old-time jukebox in the corner. Jamie hadn't thought about the place in years. "I didn't know they were still in business."

"I happened to be driving down Forty-third recently and I saw it. It brought back a lot of old memories. If you'd rather meet somewhere else…"

"No, The Cookie Jar sounds like fun. I'll meet you there at…how about seven? Right after dinner."

"Fine. Seven. I'll buy you a chocolate sundae for dessert."

Despite everything she'd been through in the last three days—the anxiety, the disappointment and the pain—Jamie found herself smiling. A few words from Rich had wiped it all away. "I'd like that."

He chuckled. "Somehow I knew you would."

A moment later, Jamie replaced the receiver and nestled back on her pillows. She'd been thoroughly chilled earlier and had piled on every blanket in the house. Suddenly she was feeling much better. Good enough to climb out of bed and make herself something to eat.

Wednesday, Rich arrived at The Cookie Jar an hour early, figuring he might as well have dinner there. He slipped into the booth with its tattered red vinyl upholstery and reached for the menu, tucked between the napkin holder and the sugar container. The menu offered four or five varieties of hamburger, in addition to sandwiches and a wide range of ice-cream desserts. He noted the picture of the chocolate sundae, the ice cream swimming in a pool of chocolate, smothered in whipped cream and crowned with a bright red cherry. Jamie's favorite.

He'd made light of discovering The Cookie Jar, claiming he *happened* to be driving down

Forty-third when he caught sight of it. That was a lie.

He'd almost gone crazy when he hadn't heard from her by Sunday evening and he'd gone out for a drive in an effort to collect his thoughts. Going past their old high school and the nearby restaurant had been no accident. He would've gone inside The Cookie Jar, but the restaurant had been closed. He wasn't entirely sure why he'd suggested they meet there. Nostalgia? A chance to remember simpler times? To relive the beginning of their friendship?

An impossibly young waitress arrived with a glass of water and a small pad, ready to take his order. Rich asked for a cheeseburger, a strawberry milkshake and an order of fries. He glanced around at the other customers, but the high school crowd had gone home and the few people there were older.

He strolled over to check out the jukebox, thinking it might be fun to hear some of the songs he'd loved in his teens. He was surprised to find he didn't recognize a single tune. Not even one. He fingered a few quarters in his pocket, but after a couple of minutes he decided not to bother and returned to the booth.

He was getting old. He hadn't really noticed

it before but he did now. When the waitress didn't look any older than twelve and he didn't recognize a single Top 40 hit, he couldn't deny it—he was past his prime.

The cheeseburger was sinfully delicious. The French fries were just the way he liked them—hot and salty. He savored the sweet, thick shake and couldn't remember a meal he'd enjoyed more.

Wrong.

No point in trying to fool himself. Any meal with Jamie would've been better. He missed her. He missed their early-morning conversations and the sound of her laughter. He missed the intimacy they shared as they talked about their child.

Their child.

Paul's three-year-old twin sons had been up and about for part of Saturday night, racing around the house in their Spider-Man pajamas. For an hour or so, Jason had played cards holding Ryan on his lap, while Rich held a squirming Ronnie. Rich had always enjoyed being with his young nephews, but he hadn't truly appreciated them until that evening. If all went well, within a year's time he'd be holding a son or daughter of his own. That had filled him with an electrified anticipation. He'd managed to contain those feelings, not knowing what was happening between him and Jamie. But he'd know soon. They were going to clear the air.

When he'd first mentioned marriage, Jamie had been afraid, full of dire predictions that sex would ruin their friendship.

He'd agreed with her then, and he did now. They were in danger of ruining everything unless they acknowledged their feelings in a mature, honest manner. Their night together had redefined their relationship, taking them from friends to lovers.

What a discovery they'd made.

What a *mess* they'd made.

He knew he should never have made love to her, but try as he might, Rich couldn't make himself regret it. If he suffered any remorse, it was that it had taken an argument to realize how much he cared for Jamie.

He'd been in love with her for years, only he hadn't known it. They'd had a special friendship all that time, and they now had a chance to have even more. Rich didn't want to say or do anything that would jeopardize their marriage *or* their friendship.

Things hadn't gone well when he'd phoned her Monday afternoon. The tension during that

call still made him wince. Rich had said none
of what he'd wanted to say, nor had he done
anything to assure her of his love. Jamie had
sounded stilted and uncertain. The conversation was over almost before it started—although at least it had ended on a lighter note.
Thank goodness for ice cream.

He'd been tempted to call her again several
times since, but decided it would be best to
wait until they could meet face-to-face. There
was less likelihood of misunderstandings that
way.

Rich had done a lot of thinking about what
he needed to tell her. First, they had to put
aside any pettiness, let go of any jealousy,
vanquish any fears. Then they'd discuss their
feelings. If the conversation went the way he
hoped it would, he'd go home with her and
spend the night.

Why not?

They were married. It didn't make sense for
Jamie to get pregnant by artificial means when
they were fully capable of doing it naturally.

Capable and eager.

He didn't plan to bring that up right away,
of course, but he planned to let her know it
was what he wanted.

During the remaining time he spent waiting for her, Rich entertained several ways of handling their discussion. Furthermore, he felt they should seriously consider moving in together. Since Jamie owned her place, it would be sensible for him to make the switch, but they'd eventually buy a house.

He was mulling over which neighborhood would suit them when Jamie walked into The Cookie Jar, wearing a full-length navy blue coat.

"Hi. I'm not late, am I?" she asked, slipping into the seat opposite him.

She looked so good. Rich had trouble keeping his eyes off her. "No…no." He summoned the waitress and asked Jamie what she'd like.

"Hot tea, please," Jamie said, smiling up at the teenager.

"Coffee for me," he told the waitress.

"You want your chocolate sundae now?" he asked.

Jamie shook her head. "No, thanks. I'm still recuperating from the flu." She folded her hands primly in her lap, her gaze avoiding his.

This wasn't as promising as Rich had hoped. "So you're still battling the bug?" Now that she mentioned it, she did look pale.

She nodded, her gaze following their waitress.

"They sure are young these days, aren't they?" he said, his eyes following hers.

She glanced at him as though she didn't understand what he meant. Rich motioned toward the teenager.

Jamie nodded, her eyebrows raised. "Pretty, too."

Rich hadn't noticed. A sixteen-year-old in braces did nothing for him. Jamie on the other hand sent his senses into orbit. All he had to do, he reminded himself, was be honest with her. Honesty led to intimacy—which led to the bedroom.

The girl brought their coffee and tea, smiling demurely. Jamie returned her smile and picked up the sugar container, shaking some into her tea and stirring it briskly. Rich couldn't remember her using sugar before, but this wasn't the time to mention it.

"I wanted to talk about what happened Friday night," he said, leaning forward, cupping the warm mug in both hands.

"Why?"

"Well, because…" He sipped his coffee before answering. Her question had caught him off guard. "It's brought another dimension into our relationship."

"H-how do you feel about…our relationship

having another dimension?" Once again she cast her gaze around the room, looking everywhere but at him.

"I think it has the potential to be good," he said, striving to sound matter-of-fact. If he let on too quickly that he was crazy in love with Jamie, he might scare her off.

"The potential to be good," she repeated, her voice so low he had to strain to hear her.

"Yes. Unfortunately we weren't able to discuss it Saturday morning." Rich watched as Jamie went stiff. He realized she hadn't liked him leaving and wondered if she'd misinterpreted the situation. He'd do his best to make amends now. "I apologize about heading out early. It might have—"

"Stop." She raised her hand.

"Stop?"

"There's no need to apologize. None. The last couple of days at home I've had plenty of time to think."

He nodded in relief. Apparently Jamie had come to the same conclusions as he had. He sipped his coffee and leaned back.

"You were right."

Rich nodded again. A man always likes to hear the truth.

"Having dinner with Floyd was an error in

judgment on my part, although it was completely innocent. After your experience with Pamela, I should've understood your feelings. As your friend…I should've been able to hear what you were really saying. If there's any blame to be placed over…over what happened, I want you to know…"

"Blame," Rich repeated. The word fired his anger, and adrenaline shot into his veins.

"Yes, I just wanted you to know I'm willing to accept the blame."

Hearing it a second time didn't improve his disposition. Rich set his mug back on the table with enough force to slosh coffee over the edges. "No one said anything about placing or accepting blame. If that's what you're here to do, I suggest we end this discussion right now."

"I was just trying to—"

"Then don't."

Jamie's gaze fell to her mug of tea, cradled between her hands. From the rise and fall of her shoulders, Rich could see how hard she was trying to avoid another argument.

He was too angry to make the effort. *Blame.* She wanted to allot blame for the most fantastic night of his life. Hers, too, but she was too proud to admit it.

Everything he'd hoped to accomplish—making this marriage real, moving in together, buying a home and creating a child, a son or daughter who'd be born from their love—seemed to disappear before his eyes. He'd longed for this meeting, hoped it would give them a way to move naturally from being friends to being lovers. Married lovers.

"I've done it again," she whispered.

"Done what?"

"Made you mad."

He knew it hadn't been her intention to offend him. Judging by the bewildered look in her eyes, she didn't understand why he felt angry.

"It's happened already, hasn't it?" Her words were so shaky, Rich half expected her to break into tears. "We've killed our friendship."

"Not necessarily." She looked pale, and here he was, furious with her, when all he wanted to do was take her in his arms.

"I *knew* this would happen," she said with a sigh. "Marriage just isn't going to work. Our feelings are all muddled up…we hardly know how to act around each other anymore."

Rich sat silent and morose. What she said was true.

"What do you suggest?" he asked after a while.

"I…I don't know. I thought I knew what I wanted. Now I'm not sure."

Rich didn't know, either. He wanted her as his wife, but he needed to be positive that she shared his feelings. What man *didn't* need that type of reassurance? It had all seemed so straightforward earlier. Now he was floundering.

"Do you feel up to walking?" he asked.

His question obviously surprised Jamie, but she nodded.

"Good." Rich reached for their tab, then left some money on the table.

They were in the old neighborhood now. The brick two-story high school they'd once attended was two blocks over. By tacit agreement they headed in that direction. Jamie wrapped a scarf around her neck and buried her hands in her pockets. Rich did the same, but he would rather have held hands with her.

They'd gone a block before either of them spoke.

"I used to think you were the handsomest boy at school."

"Me?" Rich laughed. "You certainly didn't let me know it."

"I couldn't. You were vain enough."

Rich smiled. "I used to wish I had as easy a time with grades as you did."

"Easy?" she repeated with a short, mocking laugh. "I worked my tail off."

"Remember our ten-year reunion?"

Jamie nodded. "You were with some blonde. You always went for blondes, didn't you?"

He ignored her remark. "You were with that guy who looked like David Letterman," he said.

"Ralph was a nice guy."

"Nice and dull." Rich didn't know why he'd bothered to bring Elaine. He'd much rather have spent the evening with Jamie. As it was, they'd danced nearly every dance together.

"At least all of Ralph's brains weren't located below his neckline."

"Speaking of which," Rich said, grinning boyishly.

Jamie whirled around to face him, her eyes spitting fire. "Don't you dare bring up the size of my bust. Don't...you dare."

Rich couldn't hold back his smile. "You're full of surprises, aren't you?"

"Did I ever mention the karate lessons I took? I learned how to disarm a man in three easy moves. Don't tempt me, Manning."

"*You* tempt me." Rich didn't know what made him say it, but now that it was out, he wasn't sorry. Jamie went still at his side, unmoving in the dim light from the street lamp. Rich raised his hand and glided his fingertips over her face. Her eyes drifted shut.

"I...don't think this is a good idea...."

He stopped her, tracing the outline of her lips with his index finger. He circled once, twice, three times....

"Why not?"

Her eyes remained closed, and she swayed toward him. Rich reached for her, pressing her close.

"There...was something I wanted to say," she whispered.

"Oh." He buried his face in her hair, inhaling its sweet scent. Rich didn't know how they could be at odds with each other when the attraction between them was this strong.

"You...you shouldn't distract me."

"Do you want me to stop?" His lips grazed the underside of her jaw. She tilted her head.

"Not yet...."

"Should I kiss you?"

"Please."

It was all the encouragement he needed. He brought his mouth to hers and wrapped his arms around her, nearly lifting her from the sidewalk. Her arms crept up his chest, pausing at his shoulders. The kissing was even better than it had been before, something Rich hadn't thought possible.

His mouth moved hungrily over hers, and when she sighed and parted her lips, he swept her mouth with his tongue. Jamie reacted with a swift intake of breath, winding her arms around his neck.

Rich had never intended to kiss her like this. Not on a public street half a block from where they'd attended school. He wanted her soft and yielding in his arms. And in his bed. Soon.

The salty taste of tears shocked him. She was crying. He pulled his mouth from hers. "Jamie, what's wrong?"

"Everything…nothing." She kissed him back, her open mouth over his. It was as sensuous as anything he'd ever known.

"You're crying."

"I know."

"Why?"

"Because you're making everything so *difficult.*"

"How am I doing that?" She remained in his embrace, his hand pressing the small of her back.

"Kissing me… You weren't supposed to do that."

"I'm not?"

"No…but don't stop."

"I don't plan to." Rich didn't need further encouragement. His kiss was urgent, filled with unleashed desire. They'd wasted precious days, hiding behind their fears. All along, they could've been rejoicing in the discovery of their love.

"Rich…"

Reluctantly, he broke off the kiss, his chest heaving. He took her hand, folding it in his own, and started back toward The Cookie Jar. "Let's get out of here."

"I…suppose we should."

"It's either that or make love to you in the middle of the street."

"Make love to me?"

Surely it was what she expected. A man didn't kiss a woman like that without her knowing what he had in mind, especially if that woman was his wife!

"But…we need to talk."

"Later." His steps were brisk. The sooner he got back to his apartment, the sooner he could kiss her again. He didn't want to give her the opportunity to change her mind.

"There's something we should talk over first."

"What? Can't it wait?

She shook her head. "I would've said it earlier.... I planned to, but then you suggested the walk and...we started kissing and now I'm more confused than ever."

He stopped at his car, unlocked the passenger door, then turned to face her. Resting his hands on her shoulders, he met her gaze, relieved to see the hunger in her eyes. "All right, Jamie, tell me whatever it is."

She brushed the tears from her cheeks, and drew in a deep, steadying breath. "Because of Friday night."

That again! "Yes?"

"I was thinking you might want to...you know?"

Rich thought he did. She was about to suggest what he'd been considering for the last few days—that they take this marriage seriously and move in together.

"If it's what you want, it's what I want," he said, brushing the hair from her face, his fingers lingering on the softness of her skin.

Her eyes closed, and she bit her trembling lower lip. "I don't know what I want anymore...and I don't think you do, either."

"Sure I do," he countered. He wanted her.

"I think we should give serious consideration to…"

"To what?"

"A divorce."

Nine

Rich jerked away from her as though he'd received an electric shock.

"A divorce!" he bellowed.

It wasn't what Jamie preferred, but she felt honor-bound to offer Rich the option. They'd broken their agreement, the promises they'd made to each other before the wedding.

The decision to make love had been mutual; nevertheless everything had changed, and they couldn't continue pretending it hadn't. Their lovemaking was so powerful, so moving, Jamie would treasure the memory all her life. Every time she thought about falling asleep, nestled against Rich, she went weak.

"A divorce," Rich repeated.

Jamie shuddered. He'd never know what it had cost her to make the offer. Jamie prayed Rich would give her some indication that

Friday night had been as meaningful and as beautiful for him as it had been for her.

"So you want a divorce?" he said, slamming the passenger door of his car.

"I...I didn't say it's what I wanted."

"Then why did you suggest it?"

"Because...well, because things are different now."

"You're right about that," he muttered. "I don't even know you anymore."

Jamie chose to ignore his outburst. "We'd agreed this was to be a marriage of convenience."

"You didn't exactly fight me off, you know."

Jamie's cheeks exploded with scalding color. "No... I didn't, but it doesn't alter the fact that we breached our agreement—and before we go on with our plans, I feel we should reevaluate our options and our commitment."

"You sound just like a banker. Cold and calculating. What's the matter? Are you afraid of a little emotion?" His eyes were seething with anger.

If Jamie thought he was furious when he'd confronted her with Floyd, his anger on Friday night paled in comparison to the fury she saw now.

"We're not teenagers anymore," she said

as calmly as her voice would allow. "We're responsible, mature adults who can make decisions based on something other than hormones."

"So Friday night was nothing more than a roll in the hay for you?"

"I didn't say that." Jamie was growing angry herself. "You're purposely misconstruing everything I've said. Friday night happened. Good or bad, it happened. We can't pretend it didn't."

"I had no intention of forgetting it or ignoring it or anything else."

"Then why did it take you until Monday afternoon to call me?" she cried. "Why did you sneak away in the middle of the night without a word? I woke up feeling like…like a one-night stand."

"You aren't the only one who was disappointed," Rich said loudly. "It wouldn't have hurt you to call me."

"You abandoned me."

"I made you feel like a one-night stand?" Rich paced the sidewalk. He rammed his fingers through his hair. "A one-night stand? That's ridiculous. We're *married!*"

"No, we're not," she argued. "Not really. I don't…"

"I've got the papers to prove it. Talk about denial! A wedding is a wedding, so don't try to add a list of qualifiers to it now."

"Those qualifiers were added *before* the ceremony."

"So you want out." He turned toward her, his face contorted with anger, his blue eyes piercing.

"I'm simply giving you the option. Our relationship has changed, and we can't act as if it hasn't."

"And I am?"

"Yes!" she shouted. "If I hadn't said anything we'd be halfway to your place by now. We both know I would've ended up spending the night, and then what?"

She didn't let him answer. "Then tomorrow morning," she resumed, answering her own question, "everything would be awkward again and there wouldn't be time to say or do anything because we'd both need to get to work."

Already Jamie could picture the scene. They'd be rushing around dressing, embarrassed and uncomfortable with each other, the way they'd been when Rich had phoned her Monday afternoon. There wouldn't be time to talk, but they'd exchange polite pleasantries while he drove her back to Forty-third Street so she could pick up her car. Then she'd have to dash home and change clothes again before going to work.

"It wouldn't have to be that way."

"But it would've been." After a few kisses neither one of them would want to talk, not when they were so eager to make love. There wouldn't be any discussion, no clear exchange of views; that was predictable. And their embarrassment the next morning would've been inevitable.

"What I don't understand is why you're throwing a divorce in my face now."

It all made sense to Jamie. "We were planning a divorce anyway, after the baby's born. There were certain stipulations, agreements we made before the wedding. That's all changed. If you're going to have second thoughts, the time is now."

"Is it me or you who's having regrets?" he demanded harshly.

"We weren't talking about me."

"Maybe we should."

"Oh, Rich, please don't."

"Don't what?"

"Try to turn everything I say around. I didn't mean to hurt or offend you. I just want this to be as clear as we can make it. Having a baby is too important a decision. We can't mix it up with egos."

"Easy to say when my ego's the one that's getting battered."

"I told you, I'm not doing it intentionally. All I want is for us to be honest with each other. If you decide you'd rather forget the whole thing, then I'll understand. Look what's happened so far! We've nearly destroyed the marriage, not to mention our friendship, and we haven't been married six weeks. This isn't going to be as simple as we thought."

Rich rubbed his hand down his face, looking confused.

A divorce *wasn't* what Jamie wanted, but she felt she had to give him the opportunity to end their plans now, before the relationship was further complicated by a child.

"I was so confident about what we were doing," he muttered.

"I…was, too." Jamie could barely stand the suspense, but she wouldn't say anything to encourage him one way or the other. They both had to be completely sure that they were doing the right thing. "Would you prefer to take a couple of days to think it over?"

Rich's gaze found hers. "Maybe I should. I thought I knew, but maybe I don't."

Disappointed, Jamie nodded. "I'll wait to hear from you then." She secured her purse strap over her shoulder and smiled. "Good night, Rich."

"'Night."

As she headed toward her car, which was parked four or five spaces from his, she struggled not to reveal any of what she was feeling. Rich surprised her by walking the short distance beside her.

"I've really made a mess of this, haven't I?" he asked. For the first time since she'd mentioned the divorce, he didn't look as though he wanted to bite her head off.

"We both have," she answered in a small voice. She tried to smile at him and failed. When they reached her car, she opened her purse, searching for her keys.

"It may not make any difference," Rich said, and his eyes burned into hers, "but I'd like you to know I had to work Saturday morning. I probably should've woken you. I assumed my singing in the shower would have—" he gave a lopsided grin "—but when it didn't, I decided to let you sleep. It was thoughtless of me not to leave a note."

"You were at work?"

Rich nodded. "When I did phone, you weren't there."

"But there wasn't any message."

He shrugged. "After what I went through on Friday, I was done with leaving messages. Anyway, you might've phoned *me*." The last remark was made as an offhand suggestion, but it didn't disguise his frustration.

"I did! But you weren't home. I didn't leave a message, either." What a fool she'd been. What fools they'd both been. Jamie wanted to groan at their stupidity.

"You phoned?" His sigh of frustration was audible.

"You did, too?" Her sigh joined his.

Jamie resisted the urge to weep. There'd been so much she'd wanted to say, and hadn't. So much she'd longed to tell him. And couldn't.

"You'll phone me...soon?" she asked, trying not to sound as anxious as she felt.

Rich nodded. One corner of his mouth lifted in a half smile. "I'll leave a message if you're not in this time."

"If you don't call me, then I'm calling you." She refused to leave room for any additional misunderstandings. Not again.

* * *

Before he realized where he was going, Rich found himself at Jason's apartment complex. He sat in the parking lot for several minutes.

When Jamie brought up the idea of divorce, he thought he'd explode. Rich couldn't remember ever being angrier in his life. Angry and hurt and confused. They were minutes away from making love, and she dropped the word as though she was talking about something casual, something unimportant.

Divorce.

At one point he'd decided there was no reasoning with her, and the best thing to do was walk away from the whole mess. Then the unexpected happened.

She'd started to make sense.

Jamie had always been the logical one. The perfectionist. Everything had to be just so. It had driven him to distraction when they were on the yearbook staff together. He should've realized that although thirteen years had passed since then, Jamie hadn't changed.

She wanted everything as clear as they could make it. Those were her words.

Rich knew what he wanted, too. He wanted her back in his bed so he could make love to her again. Naturally he didn't say as much.

How could he? She claimed that they were denying what had happened, that they couldn't pretend nothing had changed when everything was different. Well…yes, that was true—and no, it wasn't.

Hours later, Rich was still sitting in his car, and he still didn't know what to make of their meeting. He needed someone to talk to, so he elected Jason, whether his brother was willing or not.

The lights were out in Jason's ground-floor apartment, but that didn't deter Rich. He leaned on the buzzer until a sliver of light shot out from under the door.

He waited until he heard the lock snap open, then stepped back.

"Rich?" His brother groaned, tying the knot in his bathrobe. "What the hell are you doing here? Do you have any idea what time it is?"

Rich checked his watch, surprised to discover it was after eleven. "I need to talk," he said, marching past Jason and into the kitchen.

A yawning Jason followed. "Is this going to take long?"

"I don't know. Why? Have you got a woman with you?"

"If I did, I wouldn't have answered the door, no matter how long you rang the bell."

Jason pulled out a kitchen chair, sat down and slouched forward over his folded arms. "In case you haven't noticed, I'm not in a talking mood."

"Don't worry, all you have to do is listen."

Rich walked over to the refrigerator and opened it. He took out two cold sodas and pushed one at his brother. "When's the last time you bought groceries?"

"I don't know. Why?"

"All you've got in there is a tin can with a fork sticking out of it."

"Dinner," Jason said, covering his yawn. He waited a moment, then gestured. "Go on… talk. I'm listening."

Now that he had the floor, so to speak, Rich couldn't figure out where to start. He wasn't ashamed of having made love to Jamie, but he wasn't sure how she'd feel if she knew he was talking to Jason about their night together.

"You need some help with this, little brother?" Jason asked, straightening and opening his soda.

"No," Rich said vehemently.

"I'll give it to you anyway. You and Jamie have succumbed to the delights of the flesh and now you don't know what to do about it."

Rich was so flabbergasted that all he

could do was stare at his brother, his mouth wide open.

Jason ignored him and guzzled half the can of soda.

"How'd you guess?"

"I knew Saturday night," Jason informed him, wiping his mouth with the back of his hand.

"How... What'd I say?"

"Nothing. I asked you if Jamie was pregnant yet, remember?"

Rich nodded. The question had hit him like a sledgehammer. Jason's curiosity was what had led Rich to call her Monday afternoon. Jamie might well be pregnant from their one night together, although she'd been quick to reassure him otherwise.

"So?" Rich asked, feigning ignorance.

"You looked so shocked and you closed up tighter than a clam. It was obvious, at least to me, that she might be 'with child,' as they say."

"It's not that simple."

"Marriage rarely is. Why do you think I've avoided it all these years? I tried to tell you before the wedding, but would you listen? Ah, no, this was different, you said. You and Jamie were friends entering into a business agreement. Nothing more and nothing less."

"I remember what I said," Rich muttered, taking another swallow. He'd been incredibly naive about this marriage. The whole thing had sounded like a great idea; he had to admit it still did. Although an even better idea was to turn their arrangement into a till-death-do-us-part marriage.

"What's the matter now?"

Rich crushed the empty aluminum can between his hands. "I just met with Jamie for the first time since… since I spent the night."

"It didn't go well?"

Rich shrugged. "Put it this way. She suggested a divorce."

"A divorce? Good grief, Rich, what did you say to the poor girl?"

Rich found it interesting that Jason immediately placed the blame on him. "Hell if I know. She came up with that all on her own. According to her, I…we changed the rules so we need to reevaluate our relationship."

Jason leaned back in his chair, its two front legs lifting from the floor. "Sounds serious. So are you reevaluating?"

"Yeah," Rich said forcefully. "I think we should throw the whole prenuptial agreement out the window and move in together."

"In other words, you want this to be a real marriage?"

"Yes. Hell, yes."

"But you don't think Jamie would go for that?"

"I don't know." He hoped she would, but he'd suffered more than one setback lately. He wasn't nearly as confident as he had been earlier.

"What are you going to do?"

"I wish I knew."

"Do you love her?"

Rich nodded without hesitation. "Like crazy." Standing, he walked over to the sink and leaned back against the counter, crossing his arms. "No one's more surprised about that than I am. I didn't have a clue that I felt anything for Jamie other than friendship. I didn't even notice how beautiful she is until recently."

"What do you plan to do about it?"

"If I knew that, I wouldn't be pounding down your door in the middle of the night." Rich's response was short-tempered, but Jason should've realized that much for himself.

"Good point." Jason rubbed the lower half of his face. "I don't suppose *sleep on it* is the kind of advice you want."

"Hey, if I could sleep, I'd be home in bed." Rich had lived alone for years, but the thought of returning to an empty apartment filled him with dread. He wanted to be with Jamie. It didn't even matter whether or not they made love; he needed her. Needed her reassurance. Needed her warmth, her laughter. Her love.

"I wish I knew what she wanted," he muttered.

"Who?"

"Who do you think?" Rich tossed his brother a scathing look. "Jamie, of course."

"Don't bite my head off."

"Then don't ask idiotic questions."

Jason yawned loudly, but Rich ignored his brother's broad hint. "She didn't give me a single indication of how she felt about it. Absolutely nothing."

"At the risk of appearing stupid," Jason said mournfully, "an indication of what?"

"The divorce." Rich frowned. "She offered it to me as an option, but when I asked what *she* wanted, she wouldn't say."

"She couldn't."

"Why not?"

"Because," Jason responded between yawns, "you'd be influenced by what she said and she wants the decision to be yours. She's a smart gal."

Rich paced the compact kitchen. "I told her I'd think everything over and get back to her."

"Then go home," Jason said, standing. "Now." He ushered Rich toward the front door. "In case you haven't noticed, I'm not exactly at my brightest, and I've got surgeries scheduled all day tomorrow. I need my sleep."

Rich brushed off his coat sleeves and chuckled. "I can take a hint."

Grinning, Jason shook his head. "No, you can't."

"Dr. Fullerton's office."

"Hello," Jamie said, her hand tightening on the receiver. "I...need to cancel my appointment with Dr. Fullerton." She gave the date and time.

"Would you like to reschedule now?"

Jamie would've liked nothing better, but not knowing what Rich would decide made that futile. "Not now, thank you. I'll call you next week."

Jamie had delayed contacting Dr. Fullerton's office all day. She'd hoped to hear from Rich early that morning. In her optimistic imagination, she'd had him phoning first thing with the assurance that he felt as strongly committed to their marriage and their child as ever.

When she hadn't heard from him by noon, she had no option but to cancel her appointment. It wasn't the end of the world. Yet she was overwhelmed by her emotions for the rest of the afternoon. She had to struggle to keep her feelings from interfering with her ability to make sound business decisions.

She'd thrown a frozen entrée into her microwave for dinner and munched on miniature marshmallows while watching a cable-TV reality dating show. So much for good eating habits or any semblance of healthy emotion. She'd sunk about as low as she could.

Jamie, normally meticulous about her clothes, didn't bother to change after work. Instead, she wandered around the condo in her suit, her blouse pulled out from the waist. Her slippers made scuffing noises as she shuffled from room to room with no real purpose or direction. She would've liked to blame her lethargy on her recent bout with the flu, but she knew otherwise.

What was really bothering her was her husband. Or rather, her lack of one. A real one. In their discussion the night before, she'd tried to be as forthright and honest with Rich as she could. She'd been careful not to hint at her feelings or preferences. She was no longer so sure she'd made the right decision. Maybe she should've mentioned, even casually, how much Rich's willingness to follow through on their agreement meant to her. Perhaps if she'd assured him she'd be a good mother, their evening might have turned out differently.

No. That would've been emotional blackmail.

She couldn't have said any of those things, any more than she could've admitted how much she loved him. Or how eager she was to explore the sensuality they'd so recently discovered.

Jamie was pacing in front of the television, clutching the plastic bag of marshmallows, when the doorbell chimed.

Her heart lurched. It could be Rich, but she was afraid to hope. More likely it was her neighbor coming to complain that the television was too loud.

Her mouth was full of marshmallows, which she attempted to swallow quickly. It didn't work, although she was chewing as fast as she could. She unlocked the door and nearly choked when Rich smiled in her direction.

"Hi."

She raised her right hand, as though she were making a pledge.

"There's something wrong with your cheeks. Have you got the mumps?"

Pointing at the bag of marshmallows, she chewed some more and swallowed a mouthful of marshmallows. "Hi," she said, her heart leaping against her ribs. "I...I wasn't expecting you."

"I know. Rather than risk leaving a message, I decided to stop over. You don't mind, do you?"

"Of course not." If he had the slightest idea how pleased she was to see him, he'd be *really* smiling instead of grinning at her with those blue eyes of his. She knew she was staring, but Jamie couldn't stop looking at Rich.

"Something doesn't smell right," he said, wrinkling his nose and sniffing the air. He walked into her kitchen, and opened the microwave. Cringing, he waved his hand in front of the now-cooked—*over*cooked—entrée.

"My dinner," she explained, stuffing the bag of marshmallows in the silverware drawer.

"I thought you'd given up on this stuff."

"I did...but I wasn't in the mood to cook tonight."

"Why not?"

"Because I had to cancel my appointment with Dr. Fullerton and I was depressed. I know I'm depressed when I crave marshmallows and turn on junk television. Life doesn't get any bleaker than that."

Rich was looking at her as though he'd never seen her before.

"Go ahead and make fun of me."

"I wouldn't dream of it."

"Sure you would." She swiped the back of her hand under her nose. "I'll have you know I didn't get into the marshmallows when I broke up with Tony."

"In other words I'm responsible for reducing you to this?"

"Not exactly. I can't blame you for *everything*. Let's just say you're responsible for my choice in TV viewing."

Rich grinned and brushed a strand of hair from her temple. "Would it help if I told you I've come to a decision?"

"Probably." She was almost afraid to hope....

Instead of telling her what he'd decided, he removed her unappetizing dinner from the microwave, carried it to the garbage can and dumped it inside.

"If you want junk food, we'll order pizza, all right?"

She nodded eagerly. The *we* part didn't escape her. Apparently he intended to stay a while, which was fine with her. More than fine.

"While we're at it, I think it would be best if you ditched the marshmallows, too."

Wordlessly she jerked open her silverware drawer and handed him her stash.

"One more thing."

"Yes?" She gazed up at him, her heart in her eyes. She tried not to let her feelings show but it was impossible.

"Why did you cancel the appointment with Dr. Fullerton?"

"Because…you know." She rubbed her palms together. "I didn't hear from you this morning—not that I expected I would. I mean, overnight was much too soon for you to make up your mind. It would've been unreasonable for me to expect anything of the sort." Jamie knew she was rambling, but she couldn't make herself stop. "My…our appointment with Dr. Fullerton is…was for tomorrow and I couldn't very well go through with the insemination process, could I?"

"You've already been through one insemination process." He seemed to enjoy reminding her of that.

"Yes, I know, but…this is different."

His mouth slanted upward, his eyes bright with laughter. "I should hope so."

"I didn't *want* to cancel the appointment."

"Any chance you can reschedule?"

"Uh…" Her eyes connected with his, her heart pounding so loudly she thought he could hear it. "Are you saying you want to stay married and have the baby and—"

"That's exactly what I want."

Jamie couldn't help herself. She let out a cry of sheer joy, threw her arms around his neck and brought his mouth down to hers.

Ten

Rich moaned in surprise and welcome as Jamie's mouth sought his. He wrapped his arms around her as she stepped deeper into his embrace. His breath—and her breath, too—was heavy, abrupt, as if they'd both been caught off guard by the power of their attraction. The power of their need.

Rich tried to discipline his response to her, but his arousal was fierce and sudden.

He wanted Jamie as he'd never wanted anyone. He *needed* her. The kiss, which had began as a spontaneous reaction of joy and excitement, quickly became a sensuous feast of desperation and desire.

Rich groaned. He couldn't stop himself. His wife was in his arms, where she belonged, where he intended to keep her.

Patience, patience, his mind chanted.

They'd make love soon, very soon and when they did, it would be a celebration of their marriage. There would be no grounds for regret or misgivings. No room for doubts. It would all come in time. *Soon,* Rich promised himself. *Soon.*

By a supreme act of will, Rich drew in a tattered, shaky breath and buried his face in her hair. "You taste of marshmallows."

"I'm sorry."

"Don't be." It demanded more control than he'd ever imagined to ease himself from her arms. "What about ordering that pizza?"

"Sure." She recovered quickly, Rich noted. Far more quickly than he did. She smiled shakily up at him. "There was a coupon in Tuesday's mail…."

"Do you want pepperoni and sausage?"

"Sounds good to me," she said over her shoulder. She moved away from him as if they'd never touched. Rich envied her ability to do so. He had difficulty disguising her effect on him.

Jamie pulled out a kitchen drawer where she maintained a small file for coupons. Once again he was astonished—although he shouldn't have been—at how organized she was. In no time, she'd located the right coupon and placed the order.

The pizza arrived promptly, thirty minutes later, and by then they were back on an even keel with each other. Rich would've liked to discuss their kiss, but didn't want to say or do anything to destroy this fragile peace. There'd be lots of time later to talk about their feelings. For now, he would bask in the warm glow of his love for Jamie and wait patiently for her to love him back.

It shouldn't take long. He didn't mean to be cocky about his attractiveness or charm, but their love would be built on the firm foundation of friendship. All he had to do was exhibit patience and tenderness. The way he figured, in a week or two he'd be confident enough to approach her with the truth about his love. By the end of the month he'd be moving in with her.

No one would fault his plan. Least of all Jamie. He'd bide his time, give her the love and attention she needed, prove that he'd be a good husband to her and a good father to their child.

If everything went according to his plans, Jamie would be pregnant long before they could see Dr. Fullerton again.

Soon the pizza box lay open on the kitchen

table. Jamie had set out plates and napkins and two cold cans of pop.

"This is delicious."

Rich agreed with a nod of his head. The pizza was excellent, but its taste couldn't compare to Jamie's kisses. In fact, he could easily become addicted to the flavor that was hers alone.

"I'll call Dr. Fullerton's office in the morning," she said casually. "I probably won't be able to get in until next month." Her eyes briefly met his, as though she was seeking his approval.

"That sounds fine to me."

Her dark eyes brightened and her hand reached for his. "We're going to make this work. We can, I know it."

"Of course we can," Rich told her. If things went the way he wanted them to, they'd soon be a family—and that was exactly how they'd stay, at least if he had anything to say about it. Jamie didn't know that yet, but she'd discover his intentions soon, and by that time she'd be as eager as he was.

The alarm blared and Jamie rolled onto her back, swung out one arm and flipped off the buzzer. The irritating noise was replaced with the gentle sounds of the soft rock station she listened to each morning.

The bed was warm and cozy and she didn't relish the thought of crawling out into the dark, cold world, especially on a Monday morning. It was far more pleasant to linger beneath layers of blankets, thinking about the good things that were happening between her and Rich.

They hadn't seen much of each other in the past week because Rich was involved in a defense project for Boeing. He'd worked three to four hours overtime every night, plus both days of the weekend. Yet he called her every day without fail, usually late in the evening.

He sounded so frustrated at not seeing her as often as he wanted. As often as *she* wanted. Jamie had done her best to pretend it didn't matter, but it did. She missed him dreadfully, although their nighttime phone conversations went a long way toward making up for that.

They were like a pair of teenagers talking on the phone. There wasn't really a lot to discuss, yet they often spent an hour or more chatting and laughing as if it had been weeks since they'd last spoken. Afterward, Jamie would spend the rest of the night swaddled in happiness.

Rich was exhausted whenever he called

her. Although he'd never said as much, she had the impression he hurried out of the office and drove straight home just so he could talk to her.

Although they hadn't actually seen each other since the week before, Jamie felt encouraged by the way their relationship was developing. They were close, closer than they'd been at any time since high school. It seemed natural for her life to be so closely entwined with his. Natural and right.

Everything was going so well for them, she thought again. Rich seemed pleased when she rescheduled her appointment with Dr. Fullerton. Jamie often fantasized about their child— boy or girl, she'd be delighted and she knew he would, too.

Stretching her arms high above her head, she yawned loudly and kicked away the covers. Although she'd prefer to laze the morning away thinking about Rich and their future, she had to shower and get ready for work.

Still yawning, she sat up and turned on the bedside lamp. The room started to sway. Jamie exhaled slowly and closed her eyes. The sensation worsened until she was forced to put her head back on the pillow. The dizziness was followed by a surge of nausea.

Apparently she was suffering from a relapse of the flu. Wasn't she?

Jason called Rich at the office early Tuesday morning. "I haven't heard from you in a while," he said, giving the reason for his call. "I thought I'd check in to see how everything's going with you and Jamie."

"Fine," Rich said, studying a design layout on his desk. He held the phone to his ear with his shoulder as he worked. "I appreciated your words of wisdom the other night." However, as Rich recalled, Jason had been more concerned with getting him out of his apartment than shedding any new light on Rich's muddled marriage.

Rich had been more shaken that night than he'd realized. The mere mention of the word *divorce* had thrown him. It had also forced him to deal with the depth of his love for Jamie and had set his determination to do everything within his power to make their marriage work.

"So things between you and Jamie are better?"

"So far, so good."

"No more talk of a divorce?"

"None." Thank God, Rich mused.

"Then you've agreed to her terms?"

"More or less." It was the terms they'd *both* agreed to—only he wanted to change the rules now. All he needed was a few days to convince Jamie how crazy she was about him. It shouldn't be that difficult, especially when he was already so much in love with her, as long as he could get a few hours free from work. Which was difficult right now, with that defense contract gearing up.

"What does 'more or less' mean?" Jason wanted to know.

"It means," Rich said, his words heavy with impatience, "that I intend to make this marriage real." He glanced around to be sure no one in the office across the hall from him could hear. This wasn't the way he wanted his fellow workers to learn he was a married man.

"How does Jamie feel about this, or—" Jason hesitated "—does she know?"

"She will soon enough." Rich had never felt more frustrated. The defense project was taking all his time; knowing he'd volunteered for it didn't help, either. He'd been single at the time, but his life had changed and he was a married man. Sort of a married man. One who longed to be a real husband to his wife.

"I don't suppose you've considered telling Mom and Dad that you're married, have you?"

Jason should've gone into police work, Rich mused. He certainly possessed interrogation skills.

"It wouldn't hurt, you know," Jason added.

Rich frowned. "Is there any reason I should tell them?"

Jason's chuckle annoyed him. "Not really," his brother said. "Just promise me you'll let me be there when you do."

Rich didn't find any humor in his teasing. "I will when the time's right." That might take longer than he'd originally planned, thanks to all the overtime he'd been putting in lately. Informing his parents that he and Jamie were married, and had been for the past six weeks, wasn't a task he relished. Of course, the longer he waited, the more offended they'd be.

"Talk to you later."

"Okay," Rich said absently, more concerned about the designs he was reviewing than the conversation with his brother. He hung up the phone and glanced at his watch. The defense project was winding down, and if the day progressed as he hoped, he'd be able to take a break this evening and visit Jamie.

Rich was so involved in the designs that he didn't notice someone standing in the doorway until he glanced up. When he did, his eyes widened with shock.

"Jamie." Her own eyes were red and glazed with tears. Yet she was smiling. Rich didn't know which emotion to respond to first. "What's wrong?"

"Oh, Rich, you won't believe what's happened," she cried, and ran toward him, arms outstretched. "You just won't believe it. I...I know I shouldn't have come here, not when you're so busy, but I had to, I simply had to."

Worried that there might be something seriously wrong with her, Rich got out of his chair and had her sit down. Then he crouched in front of her, holding the armrests, forming a protective barricade around her.

"Tell me," he said tenderly.

"I woke up sick yesterday," she muttered, opening her purse and digging through it for a tissue. When she found one, she dabbed at the corners of her eyes. Once again she was smiling broadly and weeping at the same time. Tears slid down her face, and her mouth trembled with some as-yet-undetermined emotion.

"I assumed it was the flu," she said, sobbing, "but I felt fine a little bit later. I didn't even *think* to mention it when you phoned last night—but this morning my stomach was queasy again and I felt light-headed, as though I was going to faint. I wasn't sure what to think until I checked the calendar."

"The calendar?"

She nodded enthusiastically.

"Jamie?" Rich was afraid to place too much significance on what she was saying—what she *seemed* to be saying. She couldn't possibly mean what he hoped she did. It was ludicrous. They'd only made love that one time.

Once again she nodded wildly. "Rich," she said, her hands gripping his. "We're pregnant."

"Pregnant," Rich repeated in a whisper, stunned. If he hadn't been clutching the sides of the chair, he would've toppled onto his backside. "Pregnant," he repeated slowly.

"I never dreamed it would happen so quickly. My temperature was only elevated a little that morning and…I didn't really think I was fertile yet, but obviously I was. Rich, oh, Rich," she sobbed joyfully. "We're going to have a baby."

"A baby." Rich stared at her. "You're sure? You've been to see Dr. Fullerton?"

"No… I bought a pregnancy test in the drugstore this morning and a few minutes later—"

"You're sure?" he asked again.

"The stick turned blue. You can't get any more positive than that."

"Blue…does that mean the baby's a boy?" His head, his heart, were racing, trying to take it all in.

Jamie laughed and hiccuped and laughed some more. "No, silly, it doesn't mean we're having a son, it means we're going to be parents."

"But we *could* be having a son," he challenged.

"Of course. Or a daughter." She threw her arms around his neck and laughed, an outpouring of joy. It was the sweetest, most poignant song he'd ever heard.

"We're pregnant," Rich said, finally—fully—taking it in. "We're really pregnant."

"Really," she said, brushing the tips of her fingers over his face. "That's what I've been trying to tell you."

"Pregnant." Slipping his arms around her waist, he stood, bringing her with him. His mouth found hers, and he kissed her the way he'd longed to do all week.

Jamie moaned. So did Rich. The kiss created a need for much more, and this was neither the time nor the place.

"Say something," she whispered, her eyes

holding his. Her hands pressed against the sides of his jaw. "Tell me you're pleased about the baby."

Everything he wanted to tell her—his joy, his excitement, the overwhelming love he felt for her—it all formed a huge lump in his throat. To his dismay, Rich couldn't utter a single word. Finally he threw back his head and released a shout that sounded like a war cry.

"Rich?" A frowning Bill Hastings appeared in his doorway.

Rich grinned and waved. He broke away from Jamie, but took her hand in his. "Hello, Bill. Have you met Jamie Manning, my wife?"

Jamie's smile grew and grew. "Jamie Warren Manning," she corrected.

"Your *wife?*" Bill frowned again, but recovered quickly. "When did this happen? You never said a word. This isn't the same Jamie Warren you...you know, is it?"

"Yup," Jamie answered for him. "I'm the one he wanted you to ask out."

"You two are *married?*"

"We'd better be," Rich said, tucking his arm around Jamie's slim waist. The time would come when that same waist would expand, her belly filled with his child. Thinking about it, he felt shaky inside. Rich hadn't realized men were susceptible to those kinds of emotions. He'd assumed they were reserved for women. His heart was full. Overflowing with a happiness so profound, it was unlike anything he'd ever experienced. His throat thickened as though he might break into tears. Rich couldn't remember the last time he'd wept. It wasn't something men did often. But knowing Jamie was pregnant with his child, his son or daughter, was enough to reduce him to tears.

"I see," Bill said slowly, clearly not seeing a thing.

"I'm pregnant," Jamie announced.

Bill grinned, then turned to Rich. "But you offered me Seahawks play-off tickets to take her to dinner, and that wasn't more than two months ago."

"You *paid* him to take me to dinner?" Jamie muttered under her breath.

"What can I say?" Rich teased. "I was young and foolish."

"This is all rather sudden, isn't it?" Bill continued, choosing to ignore the whispered conversation between Rich and Jamie.

"Not really," Rich answered. "We've had a fourteen-year courtship."

"Fourteen years!" Bill looked astonished. "It

seems congratulations are in order. I'm very pleased for you both."

"Thank you," Jamie returned graciously.

Bill left the office then, and Jamie whirled around to face Rich. "You told him we're married!" she cried.

"You mean we're not?"

"Rich, we can't tell your coworkers and not our families."

Rich hadn't given the matter much thought. It had happened spontaneously. But if a husband had just learned he was about to become a father, he should be able to tell someone, and in this case Bill was that someone.

"Since you told Bill," Jamie said, pacing his office, "then I should be able to tell someone, too. Agreed?"

"Agreed." Personally Rich could see no harm in letting the news out. Especially when revealing the truth might actually help him achieve his goal.

Jamie reached for his phone, hesitated momentarily, then sighed deeply and punched out a phone number. Rich had no idea who she was calling. It didn't matter.

While she was waiting for whomever she'd phoned to answer, Rich moved behind her and slipped his arms around her waist. He closed his eyes and reveled in the emotion he experienced as he held her tight. He wondered how long this euphoric feeling would last. All day? A week? A month? Deep down, he began to doubt it would ever entirely leave him.

So this was love. This feeling of warmth and fullness. The sensual alertness. This knowledge that the woman you loved more than life itself was giving birth to your child.

Rich rubbed his cheek against the side of her neck. She smelled of wildflowers and spring.

"Mom, it's Jamie."

Rich tensed. She'd asked to tell one person and she'd decided to tell *her mother*. Rich didn't know Doris Warren well, but what he did remember of her wasn't reassuring. She loved to gossip. Except she didn't call it that, as he recalled. Doris *networked*.

"Jamie," Rich whispered in her ear. "You're sure you want to do this?"

"Mom, I'm calling because I've got some fabulous news."

"Jamie?" Rich was in a panic.

"I'm pregnant."

He couldn't hear Doris's response, but he knew from the loud, squeaking sound that came from the receiver that Jamie's mother was more than a little surprised.

"The father?" Jamie repeated. She twisted around and grinned sheepishly up at Rich. "That's not important. What *is* important is that after all these years, you're finally going to be a grandmother."

"Go ahead and tell her," Rich whispered. Good news, especially news this wonderful, was meant to be shared. Now that Jamie was pregnant—and now that the situation between them had changed—Rich certainly didn't plan to maintain the confidentiality of their marriage. He couldn't see the point. He was too proud to keep Jamie's pregnancy a secret.

"Yes, Mother," Jamie returned, nodding absently. "Of course, I will. No…no, not yet."

Listening to only one half of the conversation put him at a distinct disadvantage, but Rich didn't mind. He was far more interested in spreading kisses along the side of Jamie's neck.

"Of course I'm sure. One of those home pregnancy tests…. Yes, Mother. Listen, I have to go now, I'm already late for work. Yes, I'll call later. Yes, I promise."

Rich's teeth caught hold of Jamie's earlobe. Her response was immediate; she went weak in his arms. Rich had never felt more powerful in his life.

"Rich," she chastised softly.

"Why didn't you tell her we're married?"

"I couldn't… Rich!" She swatted him playfully, but he couldn't make himself stop nibbling her neck.

"Why couldn't you tell her?"

"I…I thought I'd break it to her gently. A little at a time."

"So you started by telling her you're pregnant?" He found her reasoning a bit irrational, which wasn't typical for Jamie.

"If I told my mother we were married, she'd say something to your parents. We both know she would. Mom's like that."

"Yeah." But somehow the prospect wasn't as intimidating as it had been when Jason had broached the subject earlier.

"It'll cause problems."

"No, it won't," Rich said. He reached for her hand and raised it to his lips, kissing her knuckles. "Because I won't let it."

Jamie glanced regretfully at her watch. "Let's discuss it later. I'm late." She seemed as reluctant to leave as Rich was to let her go.

"Meet me for dinner tonight?" Rich intended to make reservations at the best restaurant in town.

"What time?" Jamie asked.

He tried to judge when he'd be finished, but he had no way of telling. "I won't know until later."

"Don't worry about it. Come to my place when you're through here and we can decide then."

Jamie left a few minutes later.

Rich didn't know how her day went, but his was a total waste. More than once he found himself staring into space, dreaming of Jamie and his child, plotting how to convince her to make their marriage real.

His day wouldn't have been so chaotic, though, if he hadn't been at meetings for much of the afternoon. He'd be taking notes, and before he realized it, his mind would wander to Jamie. He wanted to spend the rest of his life with her, not a few stolen moments out of a hectic work schedule. At the end of the day, he longed to hurry home and find her waiting for him. It was easy to envision walking in the front door after a long day at the office and having Jamie there to greet him. Jamie and their son.

That warm feeling returned, and Rich knew he'd been lost in another world again. Luckily, he hadn't embarrassed himself at any of the meetings.

At seven that evening, when he'd finished at the office, he hurried out the door. Bill and a couple of the other engineers invited him for a drink, but Rich declined. He knew they were eager to hear the details of his marriage, but he was in too much of a rush to get home.

Home to Jamie and his new life. His real life. Now all he had to do was convince her how much he loved her....

Jamie opened the door and smiled.

"Hi."

If he didn't know better he'd say she seemed almost shy. "Hi, yourself. How are you feeling?"

"The truth?"

Rich nodded. Of course he wanted the truth. He remembered she'd told him about the dizzy spells and nausea attacks. He'd listened, but in his excitement had forgotten.

"Don't look so worried," she said, laughing gently. "I feel fabulous. Wonderful. I've been walking on air all day."

"Me, too."

"I should never have told my mother, though," she muttered.

If he didn't kiss her soon, Rich decided, he might lose his mind. "Why's that?" he asked, although he agreed with the sentiment.

Not giving her a chance to answer, he took her in his arms. His mouth met hers, and they strained against each other. Eager. Hungry. The kiss moist and hot. Before he could question the wisdom of his actions, he was unfastening her blouse. He'd freed four tiny buttons before he had the presence of mind to hesitate.

"Rich?"

"Do you want me to stop?"

"I...don't know."

His hand cupped her breast, which was sheathed in a pale cream teddy.

"I thought you'd be starved by now," she murmured hoarsely.

"I am," he said, kissing her once more. Slowly. Thoroughly. Until there could be no doubt of what he wanted. "But it's you I'm hungry for."

"What...about dinner?"

"Later," he whispered, easing the silk blouse from her shoulders and reaching for the zipper at the back of her skirt. "I need you, Jamie."

"I need you, too. Oh, Rich, I need you so much." Her voice was a fleeting whisper.

Rich tracked a row of kisses down the side of her neck. "Is this what you want?"

"Yes…"

He dipped his tongue into the hollow of her throat. "How about this?"

"Yes…"

He eased the straps from her teddy over her shoulders, blazing a trail of warm, moist kisses toward her breast.

The sound of the doorbell went through him like an electric shock.

Jamie tensed. "I…I'm not expecting anyone," she said, picking up her blouse and pulling it on.

"Don't answer it," Rich said urgently.

Whoever was at the door must have heard him because the buzzer sounded again in a long, angry blast.

"I'll get rid of whoever it is," she muttered, buttoning her blouse as fast as her fingers would cooperate. She hurried to the door and checked the peephole, then groaned.

"Who is it?" Rich demanded.

Jamie closed her eyes. "My mother."

Eleven

"What are we going to do?" Jamie cried, looking at Rich. She'd been an idiot to announce her pregnancy to her mother, but Jamie had been so excited and happy. Keeping such wonderful news to herself for even a minute longer than necessary was just too hard. Rich had apparently felt the same way, because he'd told a coworker.

They'd both agreed weeks before not to tell anyone about their marriage *or* the pregnancy until Jamie was five or six months along and her condition was obvious. All of that had flown out the proverbial window when Bill Hastings had stepped into Rich's office.

If Rich had found it necessary to announce their marriage, then surely she was entitled to tell someone about the pregnancy. So Jamie had done what came naturally; she'd called her mother.

"I don't think we have much of an option," Rich said calmly. "Open the door."

"But…" Once again the doorbell buzzed, now in short bursts. There wasn't time to argue, but the prospect of facing her mother filled Jamie with dread.

She opened the door. "Mother," she said, her voice unnaturally high. "This is a pleasant surprise."

Doris Warren's face revealed dismay. Slowly her gaze traveled to Rich, her eyes widening.

"Hello, Mrs. Warren," Rich said.

"Rich." She nodded stiffly in his direction, then turned to Jamie, her mouth tightening. "You didn't return a single one of my calls, Jamie Marie Warren."

Her mother had called the bank a total of seven times. With uncanny luck, Jamie had managed to avoid speaking to her. However, she was pragmatic enough to realize she'd need to soon. But first she had to talk to Rich so they could decide how much to explain. That hadn't been possible with Rich tied up in meetings all afternoon.

She'd arrived home, eager to see her husband. Her phone had rung three separate times and she'd let the caller leave messages. Not surprisingly, all three were from her determined mother. Jamie hated having to avoid her, but it was necessary until she'd had the chance to talk to Rich. Now the matter had been taken out of her hands.

"Perhaps we should all sit down," Rich suggested, gesturing toward the couch.

"I…don't know if I can," Doris Warren muttered. She immediately collapsed onto the sofa. "I can't remember when I've ever spent a more distressing day. How could you do such a thing to me?" she asked, glaring at Jamie. "I'm beside myself. My only daughter's having a baby! My only child…" She paused. "You're *sure* of this?"

"Yes, Mom, I'm pregnant."

"Who's the father?" It was more than obvious that she suspected Rich, as once again, her narrowed gaze traveled to him.

"I am," Rich announced proudly. He smiled over at Jamie and reached for her hand, squeezing it reassuringly.

Jamie was in the recliner, and Rich sat on the arm, his hand continuing to hold hers.

"There's no need for concern, Mrs. Warren," he began.

"No need for concern!" Jamie's mother shot

back. "I can tell you right now, I most certainly am concerned. This is my daughter you've been fooling around with, and I insist—no, I *demand* you do the honorable thing."

"Mother!" Jamie had never seen her mother more agitated. "Rich isn't a criminal. In case you've forgotten, it takes two to make a baby."

"I did seduce you," Rich delighted in reminding her.

Jamie frowned back at him. "You did not."

"See," Doris cried, "he admits it!"

"What would you like me to do now, Mrs. Warren?" Rich asked, seeming genuinely contrite.

If Jamie didn't know better, she'd think he was enjoying this.

"I insist you marry Jamie, of course."

"But are you sure you want me for a son-in-law?"

"I— Yes!"

"Rich!" Jamie was growing angry at this silly game of his.

Rich's fingers tightened around hers. Although he did a valiant job of trying to disguise a smile, he failed miserably. His lips quivered and his eyes fairly sparkled. "I believe we should tell her, darling."

Darling! Jamie couldn't remember Rich

using that term even once. She looked up at him, astonished by his nerve.

"Tell me what?" Doris asked.

"It's complicated." Jamie decided to lead into her marriage slowly, giving her mother time to adjust to one shock before hitting her with another.

"Life is always complicated," Doris countered, pinching the bridge of her nose.

"Rich and I have been friends for years."

"The very best of friends," Rich added.

"That much is evident." Jamie's mother raised her chin a notch, as though she needed a great deal of restraint to remain civil.

"Not evident yet," Rich said, "but it will be soon."

"What are you doing?" Jamie muttered under her breath.

"Explaining," Rich answered. Then, turning to his mother-in-law, he smiled serenely down at Jamie and said, "There's no need to worry, Mrs. Warren. Jamie and I are already married."

"*What?*" Doris sprang to her feet. "Jamie, is this true?"

"Yes," she admitted reluctantly. "But I'd hoped to break the news to you a little more gently." She frowned at Rich, not bothering to hide her irritation.

Her mother sat back down and pressed her hand over her heart. "The two of you are married.... When?"

"Several weeks ago," Rich said.

"You didn't say *anything*—not even to your own mother." This was directed at Jamie.

"There's a perfectly logical explanation...."

"I can already guess." Doris's hand flew out, her index finger pointed accusingly at Rich. "The two of you *had* to get married."

"That's ridiculous! No one *has* to marry in this day and age." Jamie felt as if she were in a tug-of-war, caught between her mother's shock and her husband's amusement. She wondered if he'd behave the same way when it came to informing his own family.

"You're right about one thing," Rich remarked. "Jamie and I did marry for the sake of the child."

"Will you stop!" Jamie vaulted to her feet.

"Darling..." Rich stared up at her blankly, as though he couldn't understand what had caused her outburst.

"Don't *darling* me!" she snapped at him, her anger getting the best of her. How Rich could find humor in this situation was beyond her. He made her pregnancy sound like…like a joke.

"Jamie, tell me what's going on here." Now it was Doris Warren's turn.

"Rich and I are married," Jamie explained, facing her mother. "I never would've agreed to the wedding if Rich hadn't insisted on it."

"I should hope he insisted."

"You don't understand, and frankly, Mother, I doubt I can explain now. Suffice it to say, I'm married and pregnant, and you needn't worry about me. I couldn't be happier." Telling her poor confused mother everything at once was sure to complicate things even more than they already were. Someday soon, Jamie would answer all her questions, but not now. Not when Rich was acting as though this had all been contrived for his amusement.

"You're happy?" Doris's bewildered gaze locked with Jamie's.

"Blissfully." It was Rich who answered for them. Jamie needed all the fortitude she could muster not to contradict him.

"Then…I'm happy, too." Doris stood, but seemed surprised to find herself on her feet. She glanced around the room as if she wasn't sure where she was. Taking the cue, Rich walked to the door and held it open.

"Shall I call you 'Mother'?"

"Ah…" Doris Warren stared up at him for an awkward moment. "If you wish."

"Goodbye then, Mother Warren. Jamie and I will be in contact with you soon."

As though in a stupor, Jamie's mother walked out the door. Rich closed it after her. The lock had barely slipped into place when Jamie turned on him.

"What do you think you were doing?" she demanded.

"Reassuring your mother." Rich walked past her and sat nonchalantly in the recliner. His actions only fuelled her anger.

"You confused her." And Jamie, as well. Just when she was beginning to believe there was a chance of something wonderful between them, he'd lapsed into these childish antics. The man obviously didn't recognize a crisis when he saw one. "What's wrong with you?" she cried, continuing to pace.

"Wrong?" His eyes went wide with a look of pure innocence.

"You made everything sound like a joke."

"The pregnancy isn't a tragedy. I couldn't be happier about it. Besides, the sooner we explained everything to your mother, the sooner she'd leave and the sooner we could get back to what we were doing and—"

"You were like this in high school, too." Jamie's anger wasn't going to be appeased that easily. Nor would she allow him to lead her into the bedroom and silence her concerns with his kisses. There was too much at stake.

"You're going to drag high school into this?"

"Life isn't one big laugh, you know."

"I never said it was."

"No," she argued, "you just act that way. We're dealing with my mother here and she has—"

"I'm not the one who told her you were pregnant."

"Oh, no," she cried, throwing her hands in the air. "You had to tell Bill Hastings instead."

"That was better than blurting it out to relatives."

"Mom would know soon enough anyway." Jamie noticed the laughter was gone from Rich's eyes and he was beginning to frown.

"If you expect me to apologize for my part in this marriage then you'll have a long wait. You've obviously got regrets, but—"

"I didn't say that."

Rich glared at her. "As I recall, you made a point of saying that *I* insisted we get married."

"You *did!*"

Rich ignored her outburst and continued without pausing. "You also insinuated you didn't want the marriage."

"I didn't." Jamie's original idea hadn't included any of this.

From the first, her instincts had told her that marriage, even a marriage of convenience, wasn't to be taken lightly. Rich had never shared her concerns and, in fact, had carelessly brushed them aside.

"The only reason I went along with this scheme of yours," she reminded him, "was because you insisted."

Anger flashed from his blue eyes. "If you're so overwhelmed with regrets, you might've said something sooner."

"I did!" She didn't want to rehash old arguments, but they'd need to clear up the past before they could deal with the future. "I tried to explain my feelings before we were married, but you refused to listen to me. You never do."

"I *never* listen to you?" he challenged.

"Okay, to be fair, you listen, then you ignore my worries and tell me how foolish they are. The wedding's a prime example of that."

"Then why did you agree to it?"

"Because…I want the baby."

"Then you should be pleased," Rich said as he marched toward the front door. "You've got your baby—it's just *me* you don't want." With that parting shot, he was gone.

He shut the door with enough force to rattle the pictures on the wall. Jamie's first instinct was to run after him and tell him she didn't mean any of it. True, she hadn't been keen on marrying him, but not for the reasons he believed. She loved him, but she couldn't let him know. She needed to remind herself repeatedly that their marriage wasn't a love match. Rich had never intended it to be. She was the one who had problems remembering that this was a marriage of convenience.

She was the one who couldn't keep her heart out of it.

Rich hadn't meant to argue with Jamie. Fighting was the last thing on his mind when he went to her apartment. From the minute she'd left his office that morning, all he could think about was making love to her again. He longed to hold her in his arms and tell her how thrilled he was about the pregnancy. But nothing had worked out the way he'd planned. Instead, they'd gotten into a shouting match during which she'd repeatedly reminded him that she hadn't wanted to marry him in the first place.

She didn't seem particularly concerned about what she was doing to his ego, either.

All right, so maybe his attitude toward Jamie's mother wasn't the best, but no way was he going to sit there wearing a frown and pretending this pregnancy was some unthinkable disaster. So he'd taken a lighter approach. If Jamie wanted to fault him for that, then fine. Guilty as charged.

He had a sense of humour. He liked to tease. Always had. A fact that Jamie delighted in reminding him. Leave it to a woman to reach back thirteen years to their high school days to dig up something they could fight about.

Rich walked across the living room, loosening his tie as he moved. So, Jamie still regretted their marriage. No wonder she'd been so eager to offer him the option of a divorce.

He lowered himself into his favorite chair, raised his feet onto the ottoman and leaned his head against the back, closing his eyes. He needed to clear his thoughts, erase any trace of pride and negative emotion. Deal with the issues facing him.

What *were* the issues?

Jamie was pregnant. Apparently she was as

thrilled at the prospect as he was himself, but for different reasons. He was a means to the end, and now that he'd accomplished what she wanted, he was of no use to her.

He felt a painful tightening in his chest. Over the years he'd met a lot of women. Women who used him, wanted him, manipulated him. He would never have believed Jamie was one of them. It was more than obvious that she was trying to push him out of her life. There wasn't much Rich could do.

He couldn't force her to love him.

Rich must have fallen asleep because the next thing he knew the phone was ringing. His eyes shot open, and he stood abruptly, awkwardly, and walked across the room. He prayed with everything in him it would be Jamie, but it wasn't his headstrong wife.

"Rich?"

This questioning, bewildered tone was one he'd rarely heard in his mother's voice. "Hello, Mom."

"I just had the most…surprising phone call from Doris Warren."

Rich groaned inwardly. "Oh?"

"She's Jamie Warren's mother."

"I know who she is."

"She told me about you and Jamie being married?" She made the statement into a question, as if she expected Rich to immediately deny everything.

"She told you that?" Circumstances being what they were, Rich chose to answer his mother's question with one of his own.

"She also said Jamie's pregnant?"

"Really?"

"Is it true?" Like Jamie, his mother had plenty of experience dealing with his stall tactics. When he didn't immediately respond, she raised her voice and asked him again. "Is it?"

Rich wearily rubbed his face, hoping that would help clear his mind. "Part of it."

"Which part?" His mother's voice was quickly advancing toward hysteria. Rich knew his father wasn't there, otherwise Eric Manning would've made the call. His mother had a tendency to get excited over the smallest details. For that matter, so did his father.

When his parents learned Taylor had married Russ Palmer in Reno, all hell had broken loose. They hadn't been thrilled to learn Christy had married Cody Franklin on the sly, either. Rich could only guess what their reaction would be when they learned he was married to Jamie. Like his two sisters, he'd married without a family wedding.

"Rather than explain everything over the phone, I suggest Jamie and I drop in tomorrow evening," Rich said. "We can discuss everything then."

"Tomorrow?"

"I should be able to get away from the office around six. I'll check with Jamie to make sure that time is convenient for her, as well."

"Just answer one question. Are you and Jamie Warren married or not?"

Rich hesitated. "Yes and no," he finally said.

"That doesn't tell me a thing," Elizabeth cried.

"I know." Rich couldn't argue with his mother about that. But he couldn't tell her what he didn't know himself.

When he'd finished the conversation, Rich stared down at the phone for a moment. He didn't have any choice; he had to call her. Swallowing his pride left a bitter taste in his mouth, but there was no avoiding it. He reached for the receiver and punched out her number.

Jamie answered on the second ring. Rich didn't bother with any greetings. "I just got a call from my mother. She apparently talked to yours."

Jamie released a slow, frustrated sigh. "I was afraid that would happen. What did you tell her?"

"As little as I could. Naturally she didn't understand, so I told her we'd come by after work tomorrow, around six, and explain." Rich tried to keep the inflection in his voice to a minimum, tried not to let any of his emotions rise to the surface.

"Tomorrow," Jamie repeated.

"If it's inconvenient, then I'll let *you* call and tell her that."

"No…I'll be there."

"I'll see you then." He knew he sounded stiff and formal, but Rich couldn't help it. A man's pride could take only so much abuse.

When he'd hung up, Rich sauntered into his kitchen. He hadn't eaten since early afternoon, but he wasn't hungry. Scanning the contents of his refrigerator, he reached for a cold pop.

On his way out of the kitchen, he paused in front of the phone. Before he could question his actions, he dialed Jason's number and waited two long rings before his older brother answered.

"Tomorrow night at six," Rich announced

without preamble. He wasn't in the mood to exchange pleasantries.

"What's happening tomorrow?" Jason demanded, clearly confused.

"I'm telling Mom and Dad I'm married."

Jason's hesitation was only slight. "What brought this on?"

"Jamie's pregnant."

"But I thought she canceled the appointment with—"

"She did." Rich realized he sounded abrupt and disagreeable. Hey, he *was* abrupt and disagreeable. But Jason had asked to be present when Rich told their parents about his marriage.

"If Jamie canceled the doctor's appointment, then how…"

"This baby was conceived in the traditional way."

Jason was silent for a moment. "You don't sound happy about it."

"I *am* happy," Rich snapped. "Real happy."

But it didn't seem a fair exchange. He wanted the baby, but nothing was happening the way he would've liked. According to Rich's plan, he and Jamie would've been in bed together right this minute. They would've been in each other's arms, her face nestled on his shoulder. When they kissed, it would've been a leisurely exploration of their need and appreciation for each other. His restless hands would be roaming at will over her body, and he'd spread his palm over her flat stomach, communicating his feelings to his unborn child. When they made love, it would've been a celebration of her pregnancy.

But Jamie didn't need him any longer.

Rich had served his purpose.

Rich had trouble keeping his mind on his work the following afternoon. Every ten minutes or so, he found himself looking at his watch. Each time, he mentally calculated how long it would be before he'd be confronting his parents with the truth.

A few minutes after five, he was sitting at his desk, reviewing some figures, when there was a polite knock at his door. He grumbled a reply, and the door slowly creaked open.

Jamie stood before him, dressed in a pretty pink suit. "Is this a bad time?"

The last person Rich expected to see waltzing through his office door was his pregnant wife.

"No," he said, rolling back his chair, "you're not disturbing a thing." Maybe his equilibrium…and his heart. But precious little else. "Sit down." He gestured toward the chair on the other side of his desk.

Jamie sat down, and he saw that her gaze fell to her clenched hands.

"What brings you here?"

"I—I thought we should discuss what we're going to tell your parents."

"What do you suggest?" He hoped to give the impression that whatever they decided didn't matter one way or the other to him. He leaned against the back of the chair and locked his fingers behind his head.

"Do they know I'm pregnant?"

"Yes. Your mother told mine."

"I thought she must have," Jamie said, with a sigh. "I feel like such a fool."

"Why?"

She shrugged, still avoiding eye contact. "For telling her. I've complicated the whole situation."

Rich didn't agree or disagree. It seemed that every time he opened his mouth, he said the wrong thing.

"How much do you think we have to explain?" Jamie asked, risking a glance in his direction.

Rich hadn't decided. "Everything," he said without giving it any thought.

"A-all of it?"

"I can't see any reason to hold any of it back." Some of the disappointment and lingering animosity from their argument from the day before seeped into his words.

"I thought we might want them to assume the baby—"

"No," Rich said forcefully.

Jamie's startled gaze connected with his. "You didn't even let me finish."

"I already knew what you were going to say. You want my parents to assume this baby was conceived artificially. I won't be a party to that."

"That *isn't* what I meant."

Rich's phone rang just then. He reached for it, although he would've preferred to ignore it.

"Engineering," he responded automatically. "Rich Manning."

"It's Paul," his eldest brother said. "I just got done talking to Mom. What's going on with you and Jamie Warren?"

"Nothing." So Mom was calling in the big guns. Paul was the responsible one in the family, or at least that was his reputation and his role. When it came to family problems, his parents tended to lean on Paul for support.

"That's not what I heard," Paul said. "I got a call from Mom no more than ten minutes ago with some crazy rumor about you being married."

"It's no rumor."

"Jamie Warren?"

"Jamie Warren Manning," Rich answered without thinking. He had to stop saying that. She'd never be a Manning. Rich could feel her stare, but he avoided glancing in her direction, refusing to give her the power to disconcert him.

"Mom says Jamie's pregnant."

"She is." Rich had no intention of hiding it. In a few months, Jamie's condition would become obvious, and while she might want to hide the truth, he had no interest in colluding with her.

"Why didn't you tell anyone?" Paul asked.

"That's a long story."

"Well, I hope you tell it tonight." Paul's disapproval was all too evident.

Rich rubbed his eyes. Thanks to Jamie, he hadn't slept well the night before. His dreams had been troubling, and he'd tossed restlessly until morning.

"Jamie and I'll be there at six. We'll explain everything then."

"Good. I'll be there, too."

Rich closed his eyes to the mounting frustration. This meeting with his parents was becoming a real spectacle, with Paul and Jason sitting on the sidelines. Rich wouldn't be surprised if his parents brought in Taylor and Christy, too.

His whole family was about to discover that Rich was the biggest fool who'd ever walked the earth.

Twelve

Both of Rich's brothers were there waiting for him when he arrived at his parents' home with Jamie at five minutes to six. Paul and Jason were perched on bar stools, holding pop cans, eager to view the latest family performance. The scene reminded Rich of one that had played out months earlier between his parents and his sister Christy when she'd announced her marriage to Cody Franklin. Rich remembered being amused by the circumstances then. Following in his youngest sister's footsteps, however, was proving to be far less entertaining.

His mother was on the phone, and from the way she was shaking her head and muttering under her breath, Rich realized she was probably talking to one of his sisters in Montana.

He walked into the living room with Jamie

beside him. He noticed how close she stood to him, which surprised him. At his office, they'd taken several minutes to review exactly what they planned to say.

To him, the entire matter was cut-and-dried. He was in his thirties, certainly old enough to do as he pleased without his parents' approval. Who and why Rich married was his own business, and that was how he intended to keep it. He'd convinced Jamie that, if necessary, he'd reveal the details of their arrangement, but he doubted it would come to that.

After Rich and Jamie were seated, Eric Manning stalked into the living room. His father was tall and in excellent physical condition; his thick hair was nearly gray, and his hairline had barely begun to recede. He was in robust health and looked it.

Rich's two sisters claimed all the men in the Manning family were black-belt chauvinists. Rich hadn't given it much thought, but he had definite ideas about a man's responsibilities—to his wife and his family.

"Rich," his father said, nodding once. Eric's face was grave, and the glance he shot Rich would have quelled Attila the Hun.

"Dad." Rich nodded, too. He chose to sit on the sofa, Jamie still at his side. He didn't know whose hand reached out first, but their fingers entwined automatically, as though they gained strength from each other. Jamie appeared far more nervous than Rich, which, he supposed, was natural.

"Your mother's talking to Taylor," his father said. "She'll be finished in a few minutes."

So Rich had guessed correctly. His mother had managed to involve his oldest sister in this.

"Would you care for something to drink?" Eric asked Jamie. "There's cold pop, coffee or tea."

"Nothing, thanks," she answered with a smile.

Rich noticed that Jamie rested her free hand against her stomach, then drew in a deep, calming breath.

"Are you feeling all right?" She'd mentioned not being well in the mornings, but he'd been so caught up in his own concerns that it had slipped his mind.

"I'm fine."

"You're looking pale."

"It's nerves," she whispered.

"What about mornings?"

Rich wasn't especially thrilled to have his two brothers and his father monitoring his conversation, but he was worried about Jamie's health and their baby's.

"My stomach's still a little queasy, but I heard it'll get better in a few months."

"The book I read says morning sickness should gradually disappear, starting at about the third month." Rich had devoured the paperback on pregnancy and childbirth in one sitting, eager to read everything he could about the changes taking place in Jamie's body. Eager to learn the most minute details about how his child was forming.

Jamie's eyes brightened. "You're reading a book?"

"It might surprise you to learn I read quite a bit," he chided.

"I know," she whispered, and her gaze met his, faltering slightly. "I guess I'm surprised you're reading one about pregnancy and childbirth."

"Why?"

She shrugged. "It just does."

That didn't say much for her view of him. Rich would have questioned her further, but his mother chose to enter the room just then. Elizabeth Manning smiled warmly in Jamie's direction, but her eyes hardened as they slid toward Rich. He didn't know what he'd done that was so terrible. His father had looked at him in much the same way, as though he should be taken out to the woodpile to have his backside tanned.

"How's Taylor?" Rich inquired conversationally, ignoring the censorious looks from both his parents. He kept his voice cool and even. He was actually proud of his composure.

"Taylor's fine. So are Russ and little Eric."

"That's great." Rich crossed his long legs and leaned against the couch. This wasn't going to be nearly as bad as he'd suspected, as long as he kept a cool head.

"Taylor's decided to do some substitute teaching for the school district. Russ isn't completely in favor of the idea, but he's coming around."

Rich knew from experience that his oldest sister's will was powerful enough to launch a rocket. Russ would do well to recognize that and act accordingly.

"She was shocked to hear about you and Jamie getting married," his mother continued, after drawing in a deep breath. "Which, I might add, came as a significant shock to your father and me, as well."

"Not me." Jason spoke for the first time. "I

knew about it from the beginning. In fact, I was Rich's best man."

Everyone's attention swung to Jason.

"You knew?" their mother echoed, accusation in her voice.

Jason nodded. "Trust me. I tried to talk him out of it, but you know how stubborn Rich can be. He refused to listen to the advice of his betters."

"You asked Jason to the ceremony and not your own *mother?*" Elizabeth Manning cried. She pulled a tissue from her pocket and dabbed at her eyes.

"It was a civil ceremony at the King County courthouse," Rich started to explain. He didn't get very far. Once again he was interrupted by his mother.

"You didn't even marry Jamie in a *church?*" Elizabeth sounded as if this was the worst misdeed of all.

"Don't be upset, Mrs. Manning, I preferred it that way," Jamie answered quietly.

"But…why get married in a courthouse when you both belong to a church?"

Jamie turned nervously to Rich. Now was the time to announce the reason for their impromptu wedding.

Rich had it all worked out in his mind. The

assurances, the brief but concise explanation of what had led to their unusual agreement. Yet when the moment arrived, Rich discovered he couldn't make himself say it.

"We did it that way for our own reasons," was all the explanation he was willing to give. From the corner of his eye, Rich caught sight of Jason arching his brows.

"According to Jamie's mother, Jamie was already pregnant at the time of the wedding," Eric bellowed. His hands clenched at his sides, he paced the length of the living room, then paused in front of the floor-to-ceiling windows, his back to Rich and Jamie. "A couple doesn't need any more reason to marry quickly than that."

"I hate to disillusion you," Rich reported calmly, "but as a matter of fact, Jamie wasn't pregnant when we got married."

Elizabeth glared at him, her expression implying it was all a lie. Rich had no intention of arguing with either of his parents; they could believe what they wished.

"Then why did Doris make a point of telling us the two of you had married because of the baby?" his mother asked.

Rich groaned inwardly. "Because we'd decided Jamie should get pregnant as soon as possible."

Jamie exchanged a look with Rich, and added, "We're married because we both want to become parents."

"I tried to tell Rich a wedding wasn't necessary," Jason inserted, "but he wouldn't listen to me. He felt that if they were going to have a baby, he should marry her first. Go figure."

His mother gave Jason a horrified look. "I should certainly hope so."

Eric turned around to face them, frowning. "Trust me, parenthood's not all it's cracked up to be."

"Come on, Dad," Paul teased. "It hasn't been so bad, now, has it?"

"When it comes to weddings," Eric argued, "it's been a nightmare. It was bad enough that your sisters had to get married on the sly—but I never suspected one of you boys would pull that stunt. I want to know when there's going to be a *real* wedding in this family."

"Diane and I had a real wedding," Paul reminded his father.

"But no one from the Manning family was there." Eric's voice boomed. "The boy goes into the army, ships out to Alaska and returns home a married man."

"It was just one of those things," Paul said, grinning.

"Getting back to Rich and Jamie," their mother said pointedly.

"By all means," Jason agreed, gesturing toward the sofa. "Let's get back to Rich and Jamie. Do you realize, Mom and Dad, that they're married and aren't even living together?"

Rich sent his brother a look hot enough to sizzle bacon.

"Rich?" His mother turned to him expectantly.

"Not living together? Why not? You're married, aren't you?" His father fired rapid questions at them. "What about—"

"We're married," Rich broke in.

"But you're not living together?"

"Not...yet." It was the best evasion Rich could come up with on such short notice. This was a subject he'd hoped to avoid, along with several others.

"They plan to move in together soon, isn't that right, Rich?" his mother asked.

"Of course." It was Jamie who responded, and Rich stared at her. He couldn't help wondering if she was sincere or if her sudden reassurances were all part of an act to appease his parents. Not that Rich had any objection to moving in with Jamie.

"Are there problems with your lease?" his mother asked next.

"Uh, I'm working on it," Rich muttered non-committally.

"I hope you'll move in with her soon," Eric asserted, burying his hands in his pants pockets. "A pregnant woman needs her husband."

"You're absolutely positive you're pregnant, Jamie, dear?" Elizabeth Manning's voice was filled with gentle concern.

"Absolutely positive," Jamie said with a firm nod. "The kit I bought at the drugstore is very reliable, but I was at the doctor's this afternoon and he confirmed it."

"You went to the doctor?" Rich asked before he could stop himself. They'd spent half an hour at his office discussing this meeting and she hadn't said a word about seeing Dr. Fullerton!

"It was a short visit."

"Did he give you a due date?"

Jamie smiled shyly and nodded.

"When?" Rich was calculating dates. His best guess placed her delivery date sometime close to Christmas. A child would be the best gift of his life.

"The last week of December," Jamie announced.

"I always did love the winter months," Rich said, having difficulty keeping the pride and elation from his voice. Then, damning caution, he brought her knuckles to his mouth and brushed his lips over her hand.

Elizabeth sighed softly. "Are you experiencing morning sickness, my dear?"

"Some."

"A husband should be with his wife," Eric reminded Rich for the second time.

"We've been talking about Rich moving in with me," Jamie said. This was news to Rich, who couldn't recall a single word of such a conversation. After Doris Warren had unexpectedly dropped by Jamie's apartment, they'd barely been able to resume their conversation.

"I've got a truck," Jason said, again motioning toward them with his pop can. "Anytime you need anything hauled, little brother, just say the word."

"I will," Rich muttered. He didn't know what Jamie was up to, but he wasn't complaining. If she wanted his family to assume this was a love match, he'd play along. From his perspective it was, so this was an unexpected turn for the better.

"It's settled, then," Eric said forcefully. "Rich is moving in with Jamie."

"Shouldn't we hold a reception in their honor?" Rich's mother asked his father. Her eyes were sparkling with excitement. Rich remembered how his mother had thrown all her efforts into the engagement party for Christy and what a disaster that had been.

"We should leave that up to these young folks, don't you think?"

Rich wasn't keen on a reception, especially in light of the fact that Jamie planned to divorce him as soon as their baby was born. Thank heaven no one had inquired too closely.

Rich made a point of glancing at his watch. "If you'll both excuse us, Jamie told her mother we'd be stopping by her house, as well." She'd delivered that tidbit of information when she'd arrived at his office earlier.

The prospect of facing Doris Warren twice in as many days didn't thrill Rich. One set of parents at a time was about all he could handle.

Jamie didn't know why she'd lied to Rich's family. Normally she stuck to the truth, believing with all her being that a lie was always wrong. Yet when Rich's father had started questioning them about their living arrangements, Jamie found herself uttering a falsehood.

Rich had looked flabbergasted when she'd said they were moving in together. Stunned. To his credit, he recovered quickly and went along with her as though they'd actually reached that decision.

Although they hadn't discussed the prospect even once, Jamie had hoped Rich *would* suggest moving in with her once he learned she was pregnant. He hadn't.

She regretted their argument of the day before. Over and over during the long sleepless night, she'd relived their angry exchange and felt worse each time.

She'd overreacted. Rich was only being Rich. She'd lashed out at him because he'd responded to a tense situation with humor.

His parting shot about her not wanting him now that she was pregnant troubled her the most. He couldn't honestly believe that, could he? Jamie was crazy about Rich. She'd been in love with him for years, but she'd been too blind to recognize it.

After her appointment with Dr. Fullerton, she'd gone to Rich's office at the Boeing Renton complex. She'd hoped they'd have a few minutes alone to clear the air. But when she arrived, Rich was stone-cold and about as friendly.

Only when they were at his parents' home did he lower his guard. He'd taken her hand in his and smiled down on her as though they'd never exchanged a cross word. Of course, it could all be for show, but Jamie prayed that wasn't the case.

"Your mother seems to be in better spirits this evening," Rich said conversationally. He drove at a relaxed pace, weaving through the narrow neighborhood streets.

"She's had time to adjust to our news." Their visit had been short and sweet. Just long enough to offer the reassurances Doris seemed to need. Jamie hadn't found that difficult, because she was perfectly comfortable in the role of happy mother-to-be.

"Have *you* adjusted to the news?" Rich asked.

"Yes. What about you?"

Rich nodded. "I suppose I should be surprised, but frankly, I'm not. By the way, are you hungry?"

"A little." Jamie was famished. She'd woken with a queasy stomach that morning and skipped breakfast. Then at noon, she'd eaten a small carton of blueberry yogurt but nothing since.

"Do you want to go to a restaurant and get something to eat?"

"No," she said, thinking quickly. "We could order pizza and have it delivered to my place."

He glanced at her, as if the suggestion had astonished him. "Sounds good to me."

It was nearly eight by the time they got to Jamie's condominium. While Rich ordered the pizza, Jamie went into her bedroom and changed out of her business suit. She chose jeans and a pale blue sweater.

When she returned to the living room, Rich had loosened his tie and was leafing through the evening paper. He looked up when she entered the room and slowly set the newspaper aside.

"I hope you realize both sets of parents expect me to move in with you now." The thought apparently weighed heavy on his mind.

"I know." She sat across from him, leaning forward, and clasped her hands. "Personally I...don't think it's such a bad idea."

"You don't?" He didn't seem to believe her.

"I mean...this will probably be the only pregnancy for either of us, and since you've been reading so much about it, and seem so interested…it's only fair that you share as much of the experience as possible." Jamie hesitated a moment. "Unless, of course, you'd rather not live with me."

He gave a noncommittal shrug. "I don't mind." His gaze moved past her to the hallway that led to the two bedrooms. "Naturally I'll be sleeping in the spare room."

"Naturally," Jamie concurred. But not for long, if everything went as she hoped. She loved Rich. Truly loved him. So far, she'd bungled their relationship and their marriage at every turn. If he were to share these short precious months with her before the birth of their child, there was a chance he might grow to love her.

It was worth the risk.

Worth the potential heartache.

Worth gambling her pride and even her future for this one opportunity.

The pizza arrived soon after, and they sat at the kitchen table, the cardboard box propped open in front of them. They both drank tall glasses of cold milk.

"So you've been feeling queasy in the mornings?" Rich posed the question after several minutes of comfortable silence. He too seemed to be working to maintain this fragile peace.

"Only a little. Dr. Fullerton said it would pass soon enough. I haven't gotten really sick."

"Good."

"Dr. Fullerton suggested I nibble on a couple of soda crackers when I wake up."

"I can bring them to you, if you like."

Jamie nodded. She *would* like that, but she was afraid to let Rich know how much it would mean to her. Even now, weeks later, she continued to miss their early-morning phone conversations. They'd shared a special closeness then, one that had gone from her life.

"Would you like a cup of coffee?" Jamie asked when they'd finished.

"Yes, please.

"Go ahead and read the paper and I'll get it for you."

"That's a nice, wifely thing to do."

"Yes, it is, isn't it?" Jamie responded with a saucy smile. She took her time making the coffee. While she waited for it to brew, she cleaned the kitchen, wiped the counters and placed their few dishes in the dishwasher.

Carrying a steaming cup of coffee into the living room, she hesitated when she saw that Rich's eyes were closed, although the paper was still clutched in his hands.

Smiling to herself, Jamie sat on the nearby

ottoman. She took a sip of the coffee as she carefully studied the man she'd married. His features were more relaxed now, his head cocked slightly to one side.

How handsome he was. His good looks were even more appealing in slumber. Not sure what dictated her actions, Jamie set the coffee aside and slipped the newspaper from his unsuspecting grasp. Rich stirred briefly, then nestled more securely in the chair.

Jamie reached for the lamp, dimming it. Then, calling herself a romantic idiot, she slipped into Rich's lap and pressed her head against his shoulder.

"Jamie?" He sounded unsure.

"Were you hoping to find someone else in your arms?" she asked in a small whisper.

"No." A smile faintly curved his mouth.

His grin disappeared as his hand framed her face, and his blue eyes held her captive. Jamie could feel her heart pound frantically. Then his thumb caressed the line of her jaw.

"I never realized how beautiful you are," he whispered. "All these years…"

Jamie dropped her gaze, afraid to meet his eyes. She wasn't anywhere close to being beautiful, and it hurt, a good kind of hurt, that he should think otherwise.

His mouth sought out hers. The kiss started slowly, gently, so gently that Jamie could feel herself begin to melt. A feeling of sublime languor filled her. It was completely unfair—downright decadent, in fact—that he could make her feel such things with a simple kiss.

Simple. Rich didn't know the meaning of the word. Certainly not when it came to kissing.

Jamie heard the whimpering sound before she was aware that it came from her.

Rich ended the kiss as leisurely as he'd begun it. Jamie's eyes remained closed, and her breathing came in staggered gasps. For long, contented moments, he held her. His fingers were at the back of her head, stroking her hair. In those moments, Jamie felt the air vibrate with sweet, unspoken promises.

He wanted to make love to her.

Jamie wanted it, too.

"I should be heading home?" Rich's voice rose softly at the end of his statement, turning it into a question.

"No," she whispered, catching his lower lip between her teeth.

"No?"

"You're moving in with me, remember?"

"Starting tonight?"

"Starting right this minute."

"You're sure?

Jamie smiled and pressed her lips to his. "You want to argue with me?" she murmured.

"No…it's just…"

She didn't allow him to finish, kissing him again, cramming her heart, her soul, her *love,* into a single kiss.

She'd surprised him; his gasp confirmed as much. He groaned anew, then deepened the kiss.

They were both trembling when it ended.

Getting off his lap, Jamie stood and held out her hand to Rich. His smoky, passion-hazed eyes met hers, his gaze questioning.

"You're sure?" he asked her again, his words hoarse with need, his eyes hot with passion and some other emotion she couldn't quite read. Restraint? Doubt? Jamie didn't know which.

"I'm sure."

"You're already pregnant."

Why he felt he had to remind her of that was beyond her. "Yes, I know." As she was speaking, her hands were unfastening the buttons on his shirt. Rich helped her by pulling his tie loose and dropping it to the carpet. Jamie slid the shirt from his shoulders, then ran her hands down the full length of his arms.

His chest captured her attention next. His warm, muscular chest. She ran her flattened hands over it, marveling at the strength she sensed in him. She closed her eyes, wanting him so badly she felt weak with the need.

"You make me crazy," he whispered.

"I do?" It made no sense to Jamie.

"Yes. I want you so much you make me ache."

"I know.... Me, too."

Rich groaned and took her in his arms, lifting her against him until she became profoundly aware of his arousal.

For one wild second it was as though the world stood still for them. Rich's blue eyes appeared aquamarine in the dim light. Bright, intense, filled with promises.

Jamie felt completely vulnerable to him. Vulnerable and desirable, more desirable than she'd ever felt in her life. She smiled and moved away from him.

Rich looked confused, but he released her.

Jamie turned and had gone two steps before she turned around again. A smile quivered at the edges of her mouth. "You coming with me?"

"Where are you going?"

She laughed softly, sexily, and held out her hand to him. "You mean you don't know?"

Thirteen

Rich woke in the middle of the night. It took him only seconds to realize he was in bed with Jamie. For the next few minutes he did nothing more than watch his wife as she slept. He drank in every delicate nuance of her beauty. He stared at her as if they'd been separated for months, years, when she'd actually spent the night in his arms.

Gradually his gaze lowered to her lips, parted slightly, her breathing slow and even. She had the most delectable mouth....

Desire came at him unexpectedly. Memories of the gentle way Jamie had led him to her bed suffused him like a mist. She'd held her arms out to him, until the ache of wanting her, needing her, dissolved any will he had to refuse her.

She'd freely opened her heart and her body

to him. When she'd cried out in pleasure at her completion, the sound of her joy had echoed in his very soul. The sheer, utter beauty of their lovemaking had marked him in ways he was only beginning to understand.

Jamie stirred and rolled her head to one side. Her hair spilled across her face, and after a moment, Rich risked waking her by gently brushing it aside. His breathing was fast, much too fast considering the simplicity of the gesture.

He leaned forward, intending to kiss her. The way he was feeling, with need clawing at his insides, he knew if he followed through with his intention, the kiss would be too intense, too powerful. By an act of will, he stopped himself just in time.

He'd made love to her only hours before and already he was wondering how long it would be before he could do so again.

He had to think. Pull himself together. Make some sense of this nagging physical ache, this overwhelming need, before he woke Jamie and frightened her. Folding back the covers, he sat on the side of the bed, rubbing his face.

"Rich."

The panic he heard in Jamie's voice made him turn around.

"Don't leave me," she pleaded. "Not again."

"I wasn't going to." He slipped back into the bed and gathered her in his arms. She felt so soft against him. Holding her, he wished he could stay like this forever.

"Don't go," she repeated, almost deliriously, clinging to him.

"I can't." Even if he'd wanted to, Rich could never have walked away from her. He was so much in love with her, so driven by need... and desire.

He kissed her, hoping to reassure her, but the kiss was everything he'd feared. And wanted. His mouth was hard and demanding, as his hands investigated her warm, perfect skin.

"Jamie..." He slid his mouth down the perfume-scented curve of her neck, down her shoulder to the peaked softness of her breast.

Jamie moaned softly and arched her back, encouraging him, plowing her fingers through his hair, thrashing beneath him.

He lifted his head and kissed her mouth. "I need you...again," he whispered.

Their need for each other was as urgent as their kisses. A strangled cry slipped from her throat as she clutched at his back.

Rich jerked his mouth from hers. "I'm scar-

ing you?" He was afraid he had, or worse, that
he was hurting her.

"No...no, love me, just love me."

"Yes. Oh, yes."

Rich intended to do a lot more than simply
fulfill their bodies' hunger. But for now, his
need was too great to take it slow. Or easy.
Ruthless desire dictated his actions.

She lay there, eager and trusting, vulnerable
to him. Her dark hair fanned about her shoulders. Her sweet face was flushed with excitement, her eyes wide and misty with an emotion
too strong to voice. Her lips were parted and
moist from his kisses, and her breath came in
tiny gasps of encouragement.

"Jamie...love. My love."

Rich couldn't resist her a second longer. Not
another second.

The alarm sounded while it was still dark.
Jamie rolled onto her side and reached blindly
for the clock radio, shutting off the irritating
noise.

Rich moved toward her, cradling her, placing his arm around her middle. "Good morning," he whispered. With familiarity, his hand
cupped her breast. Although they'd spent much

of the night making love, Jamie was astonished by her body's ready response to his touch.

"Morning." Jamie couldn't help feeling a little shy after the tempestuous night they'd spent. Memories of their lovemaking filled her mind—the brazen way she'd led him into her bedroom, stripped for him, stripped him, sent a surge of color into her cheeks.

"How are you feeling this morning?" Rich asked, his mouth close to her ear. He caught her lobe between his teeth and sucked gently, shooting warm shivers down Jamie's spine.

"I'm…fine."

"Do you want me to bring you some crackers?"

Jamie hadn't immediately realized he was asking about the baby, the pregnancy. "Not… yet." She eased back the covers and cautiously righted herself. When she did suffer bouts of nausea, it was generally when she first sat up. With her legs dangling over the bed, she inhaled a deep breath and was relieved to discover she didn't feel queasy at all.

"Do you want to shower first?" Rich asked from behind her, his hands at her waist.

"Please." She had trouble looking at him. It was silly to be so nervous, she told herself. They were married, for heaven's sake. Married. There was no reason to feel uncomfortable or ill at ease. Rich was her husband, and he had a perfect right to spend the night with her.

Jamie moved into her bathroom and turned on the shower, adjusting its temperature. It wasn't until she was under the pulsing spray that she remembered.

The scene replayed itself, its effect as brutal as a slap across the face.

Rich had been about to leave her again, sneaking out in the middle of the night. If she hadn't half wakened when she did, he would've walked out on her a second time. Once again he'd planned to leave her, to let her face the empty morning alone. Except that this time she'd pleaded with him to stay.

Jamie didn't know how long she stood under the spray. Long enough to regulate her breathing and wait for the pain that rippled through her to subside.

When she finished, she forced a smile and walked nonchalantly back into the bedroom, a white towel around her. "Your turn," she told him, not meeting his eyes.

Rich had made coffee and brought her a mug, as well as a small plate with four soda crackers. "Breakfast is served," he said, bowing before her.

Jamie drank some of her coffee, careful to keep the towel securely in place with one hand. It was ludicrous to act modest after what they'd shared. The things they'd said. The things they'd done. Beautiful things...

Nevertheless she was.

Rich frowned, then left her. Although the bathroom door was shut, Jamie heard him singing at the top of his lungs over the sound of the shower. She took advantage of the brief privacy to get dressed, haphazardly choosing her outfit for the day.

She made the bed, folded Rich's scattered clothes and laid them on top, then hurriedly moved into the kitchen. Generally she didn't pack a lunch for work, but she did this morning, just to pass the time. If there was anything to be grateful for, it was that Rich hadn't called her *darling*. He'd only done that in the presence of others, for the sake of the pretense they had to maintain in front of their parents.

She was putting together a sandwich when Rich joined her. He poured himself a second cup of coffee. Jamie concentrated on making her turkey sandwich and managed to avoid eye contact.

She turned around to get an apple from the refrigerator and stopped short of colliding with Rich. "Oh, sorry," she mumbled under her breath, flattening herself against the counter so he could step past her.

"Would you like some breakfast?" she asked matter-of-factly, as though she often made the same inquiry of men who spent the night with her.

"Just coffee, thanks."

Jamie sighed with relief. The intimacy of cooking a meal for him would've been a strain. She made a point of glancing at her watch. "I guess I'd better head out to the salt mines," she said, striving to sound carefree and happy when all the while there was a lump in her throat that made it hard to speak.

"Me, too." Rich's voice was low and hesitant, as if he wasn't quite sure what was happening, but whatever it was, he didn't like it.

Jamie didn't, either, but she didn't know what to do about it.

She was halfway out of the kitchen when Rich stopped her.

"I'll have to leave with you."

"Why?" She was eager to escape, to be by herself, examine her thoughts and reactions, analyze their relationship.

His smile didn't quite reach his eyes. "I don't have a key to lock up with."

"Oh, right." She opened the closet and pulled out her coat.

"If I'm going to move in with you, we should have an extra one made."

"Move in with me..." She'd suggested it when they'd met with Rich's family. It had seemed like a good idea at the time, and she'd been so eager to find a way to make her marriage work.

"I take it you've changed your mind?"

"No," she said hastily. "I...just think we should reevaluate the situation before we do something we might regret later."

"'Regret later,'" Rich repeated slowly. "In other words, you regret having made the offer."

"I didn't say that."

"You didn't have to." He moved past her and out the front door, slamming it behind him. The sound reverberated like thunder, leaving Jamie alone to withstand the storm.

Rich had never met a more contrary woman in his life. It seemed that one minute she was leading him into her bedroom, and in the next she was behaving as though she couldn't get away from him fast enough.

Rich wasn't the one who'd announced to his family that they were moving in together. Nor had he invited himself into her home for dinner and then seduced her. It was the other way around. All right, she hadn't exactly seduced him, but the lovemaking had been Jamie's idea.

Then, in the light of day, she'd acted as if she'd never seen him before. As if she would've preferred that he disappear in the middle of the night.

Leaving before she woke was what had gotten him into trouble the *first* time they'd made love.

Rich was damned if he did and damned if he didn't.

He didn't understand it. He'd never been this confused by a woman.

Although Rich tried to work, by midafternoon he felt like calling it quits. Leaning back in his chair, he rubbed his tired eyes. Generally, when he had a problem he wanted to talk over with someone, he called Jason. The two of them had been each other's support system for years.

This time, however, Rich decided to phone Paul instead. Paul had been married nearly five years; surely in all that time he'd gleaned *some* wisdom about women and marriage.

Rich stood and closed his office door before sitting back down and reaching for his phone. Paul worked for the largest of the two Seattle papers and was often out chasing down a story. But his brother answered the phone.

"Got a minute?"

"Sure," Paul teased. "The only pressing thing I have is a three o'clock deadline."

Since it was a quarter to three, Rich figured he'd better talk fast. "Did Jason tell you about Jamie and me?"

"Not exactly," Paul said, his amusement evident in his voice, "but I put two and two together. Jason confirmed my suspicions, although I have to admit I would never have guessed you'd agree to artificial insemination."

"It didn't work out that way."

"That's what Jason said."

Rich could picture his brother in the middle of the newsroom, leaning back in his chair wearing that cocky know-it-all grin.

"What can I do for you?"

"Explain something to me."

"If I can."

"Women. And how they think."

Paul responded with a low laugh. "You want me to explain a woman's mind. I hope you're kidding. No one, at least no man, will *ever* be able to understand the way a woman thinks. Trust me, I've got five years' experience in this marriage business. If you don't believe me, ask Dad. He'll tell you the same thing. Take Diane. She wants another baby. Apparently she isn't busy enough with Ryan and Ronnie. For weeks on end she's talked about nothing else. She wants a little girl, she says. The twins run her ragged as it is. Besides, there's no guarantee we'd have a girl. We actually had a big fight about it last week."

"And?" Rich didn't mean to pry, but he was curious to know how Paul and his wife settled their disagreements.

"Well, I stood my ground, if that's what you mean. Not that it did much good," he admitted reluctantly. "I absolutely refused to discuss having another child. I tried to appease her though, I don't want to be dictatorial or unreasonable. I said we'd talk about it this time next year. That way the twins will be in kindergarten when the new baby's born. Planning our family makes sense to me."

"What did Diane say?"

"Nothing." This was followed by a significant pause. "But I should mention that she threw out her birth-control pills."

"Is she always this stubborn?"

"It's not just Diane. All women are stubborn. To make matters worse, she wore this sexy little piece of black lace to bed. I tried to ignore her, pretend I didn't see…you don't need me to tell you what I *could* see."

"No, I don't." Rich would rather not hear. He still didn't know what to make of Jamie's actions that morning. Had he frightened her, wanting her the way he did? Hell, it hadn't seemed like it the night before, but what did he know?

Apparently very little.

"The thing is, Diane will probably get her way simply because I don't have the strength to fight her. I could stop making love to her, but then I'd be the one losing out."

Rich rubbed the back of his neck. "Does Diane ever say one thing when she means another?"

Paul's laugh was abrupt. "Oh, yeah. In my experience, women are often indirect. They figure they're being subtle or giving us hints or something like that. But they won't come right out and say what they want. Oh, no, a man's supposed to guess, and heaven forbid if we guess wrong."

Rich exhaled a long, slow sigh. Paul was confirming what he already knew. "Remember, when we met with Mom and Dad, how Jamie casually said I was moving in with her?"

"Yeah."

"It sure surprised me when she brought it up. We'd never said a word about it."

"You mean you don't want to move in with her?"

"Of course I do! For weeks I've been trying to figure out how to suggest it. Then, out of nowhere, she invites me to live with her, in front of my family. I was so excited it was all I could do not to jump up and somersault across the living room floor."

"So what's the problem?"

It was a logical question and one Rich couldn't answer. "If I knew that, I wouldn't be calling you."

"All right," Paul said. "Start at the beginning."

"I drove home with Jamie last night."

"And?" Paul prompted when Rich didn't immediately continue.

"And I ended up staying the night."

"Everything sounds fine to me."

"It was—until this morning."

"What happened then?"

Rich shrugged, although Paul couldn't see him. "I can't say. The alarm went off and we were cuddling like old married folks. Ten minutes later, Jamie's out of the shower, with this towel wrapped around her middle. She wouldn't so much as look at me. I played it cool, gave her some space. Some women are modest—I understand that—so I left her alone.

"Before I know it, she's in the kitchen making herself lunch like it's the most important thing she's ever done. By accident I happened to step too close to her and she practically threw herself against the counter so we wouldn't touch." Rich paused to take a deep breath. "On top of that, when I said I should get a key to her place, she tells me we should reevaluate my moving in with her."

"I see," Paul muttered.

"What'd I do wrong?"

"*Something,* that's for damn sure. Think," Paul advised. "You must've made some remark that set her off."

"Like what?" They'd done more kissing than talking.

"How should I know? I wasn't there. Just think… review everything you said."

"I've tried that, but I can't come up with a single thing I could have done to warrant this reaction."

"Then ask her."

"I can do that?"

"Yeah," Paul said, but he didn't sound convincing. "It's not the best procedure because… well, you'll learn that soon enough. But if you're honestly in the dark about what went wrong, then you might as well ask. But if you do, be prepared."

"For what?"

"To have your ego shredded. When Diane acts like that, I know I'm in trouble. Often, and this is what's so confusing, Diane can't even tell me what I did. All she knows is that she's furious with me."

"She can't explain why she's mad?" Rich could hardly believe it.

"It's true. She glares at me like I should be arrested. Then, when I can't stand it anymore, I finally ask her what I did that was so terrible."

"And?"

"And," Paul added with a sigh, "she says she's still getting in touch with her feelings. According to her, it has to do with her upbringing."

"How?"

"Well, the way she was brought up, according to her, was all about being taught never to make a fuss or create waves. To be a 'good girl,' which means not to make any demands."

"I see."

"So what are you going to do?"

Rich hesitated. "What you suggest. Ask her."

"You're a good man, Rich Manning," Paul said, as if Rich should be awarded a medal for bravery. "Let me know how it goes."

"I will," he promised. After thanking his oldest brother for the advice, Rich hung up, resolved to bring the situation into the open as soon as he had the chance.

The rest of the afternoon passed in a blur. Because they were putting the finishing touches on the defense project, Rich had to stay late that night. He wasn't pleased about it, but he had no choice. Bill Hastings and the others were working overtime, as well. Rich couldn't very well announce that he'd had an argument with his wife and then leave. Especially when half his colleagues didn't even know he *had* a wife.

At quarter past six, there was a polite knock at his door. He glanced up and did a double take when he saw Jamie standing there.

"Can I come in?" she asked shyly.

"Of course." He stood and gestured toward the chair on the opposite side of his desk. Once she sat down, he did, too. This was the chance he'd been hoping for, but since she was the one who'd come to see him, Rich figured he'd let her start the conversation. Trying to appear as nonchalant as possible, he leaned back in his chair and crossed his legs.

"I want to apologize for this morning," she said in a small voice.

"Thank you." Rich was in a generous mood. Apparently she'd seen the error of her ways and had come to make amends. He felt a surge of relief. Maybe this was going to be easier than he'd expected.

"I…I was completely unreasonable."

"Does this mean you want me to move in with you, after all?"

"Yes, of course…that is, if you're still willing."

Was he ever! "It's certainly something to think about," he said solemnly. Then he added,

"I read that women are often unreasonable during pregnancy."

"Your book said that?" Jamie asked, frowning.

He nodded. "It's all those hormones."

"I bought a book, too, but I haven't got to that chapter yet. It makes sense, though." She opened her purse and reached for her wallet, snapping open the change compartment. "I had a key made for you during my lunch hour," she said, handing it to him.

"I'm working late this evening." He hoped she'd suggest he drop in at her place—at *their* place—on his way to the apartment.

"I thought you might be. That's why I came here first."

A short uncomfortable silence passed. Rich wondered if he should raise the subject of her bad mood this morning or let it go. Maybe it was simply the hormonal overload. Or maybe she didn't even know herself and regretted her reaction.

"I was thinking I'd bring some of my clothes over this evening," Rich said, experimentally, waiting to see if she'd offer him some encouragement.

"That would be fine."

It wasn't encouragement, exactly, but it wasn't opposition, either.

"I'll contact Jason and ask if he can help me move the furniture and the large items this weekend." He'd put what he didn't need into storage.

"I'll make sure there's plenty of room for your stuff." Jamie stood up. "I guess I'd better leave."

"One last thing."

"Yes?"

When Rich got to her place, he didn't want to play any guessing games about their sleeping arrangements. "Where will I be sleeping?"

Jamie's eyes widened at the directness of his question. "Uh…that's up to you."

"No, it's not," he returned firmly. "It's completely up to you."

"Anyplace you'd like," she said almost flippantly.

"Where would you *like* me to sleep?" he asked, throwing the question back at her.

She hesitated, then lowered her gaze. "With me."

He felt as though he'd scaled the gates of paradise. "There isn't anyplace else I'd rather sleep," he said, unable to keep the pleasure from his voice. He got to his feet and walked toward her, slipping an arm around her shoulders. Rich walked her to the elevator, and while they waited, he leaned forward and gently kissed her.

As so often happened during their kisses, Rich found himself wanting more. Much more. She braced her hands against his chest, her breath ragged, uneven. A warmth filled his heart and seemed to radiate outward.

When they broke off the kiss, Rich was delighted to see that Jamie was trembling. For that matter, so was he.

"You make me forget," she said in a husky whisper.

Rich understood. She made him forget where he was, too.

Bill Hastings strolled by and smiled affectionately at them. He stood a discreet distance away, apparently hoping to talk to Rich.

The elevator arrived and although Rich was reluctant to let her go, he still had another hour, at least, of work.

"Goodbye, darling," Rich said. "I'll be home in a couple of hours."

Jamie's reaction was instantaneous. She tore away from him, stepped into the elevator and whirled around. Her eyes, her beautiful dark eyes, were brimming with tears.

"That's the most horrible thing you've ever said to me, Rich Manning."

Rich was so mystified by her irrational behavior that it took him a moment to respond. "What I said? What did I say?"

"You know very well." With that, the elevator doors glided shut.

Fourteen

"What'd I say?" Rich asked, utterly bewildered. He turned to his coworker, at a loss to understand.

Bill Hastings's blank look confirmed that he was equally in the dark.

"Whatever it was must've been awful. Jamie was crying."

"I don't *know* what I said," Rich told him, baffled.

"Maybe she's upset because you told her you wouldn't be home for a couple of hours."

Rich shook his head. "Maybe…" Although his working overtime had never seemed to bother Jamie before. Not that he was aware of, anyway. Sighing with frustration, Rich decided to give up trying to figure out his wife. Jamie had been a whole lot easier to understand before he married her, back when they were just friends.

"Leave now," Bill urged. "Sort this out before it's too late." That meant he was offering to handle the brunt of the remaining paperwork himself, which Rich didn't think was fair.

He shook his head again. "I'll work it out with her later."

"You're sure?"

"Positive."

Bill hesitated. "Maybe you should reconsider." Bill gave him a look that reminded Rich his friend was divorced. He knew that Bill wished his circumstances were different. Over a beer one night, he'd told Rich that if he had it to do over again, he'd work harder to save his marriage.

Rich's heart was racing. "You don't mind?"

"Not at all. Go! Do what you have to before everything gets blown all out of proportion."

"Thanks," Rich said over his shoulder. "I owe you one."

"Don't mention it…. Only, Rich?"

"Yeah?"

"Be happy."

Rich nodded. "I intend to, even if it kills

me." Remembering the furious glare Jamie had sent his way, he figured it probably would.

Although he hurried out of the building and toward guest parking, Rich missed her. Jamie's car was nowhere in sight. He released a breath of frustration as he turned and walked to the employee parking area.

Maybe it was better that he hadn't caught up with her. His mood wasn't too positive at the moment, any more than hers was. Would married life always be this difficult? he wondered. Would his life consist of continually making amends for some unexplained wrong? Must he be constantly on his guard, afraid to speak his mind?

If there'd been something handy to punch, Rich would've done it. Plowing his fist into empty air only discouraged him more.

How fitting. Fighting imaginary ghosts. Didn't that describe his entire marriage?

Jamie had always been a sensible woman, or she had until she'd become pregnant. Yes, he'd read pregnant women could be temperamental, but this was ridiculous.

Jamie felt like a fool. Tears had left moist trails down her cheeks. She wasn't a woman given to such blatant emotion, and her actions surprised her even more than they did Rich.

But he deserved it, she thought in quick reversal. Calling her *darling* in front of his friend, putting on a big show, pretending to love her. As if saying it wasn't enough, he had to go and wear a besotted look, as though parting was such sweet sorrow.

It all seemed to be a game with him, and she couldn't bear to play anymore. If this was the first time, she might've been able to overlook it, but this nonsense had become a habit. When they'd gone to visit his parents, Rich had sat beside her, his hand clutching hers. The tender expression on his face, the loving way he'd smiled down on her, was more than she could stand.

It was all so hypocritical. Counterfeit love.

Would she ever learn? Men were fickle, not to be trusted. And yet she knew Rich, probably better than she did any other man she'd ever dated. His behavior surprised her. More than that, it hurt.

Driving while crying wasn't safe, so Jamie pulled over to the side, got a tissue from her purse and blew her nose. When she could see clearly again, she sniffled and continued driving.

Once she was home, she wandered around her condo, walking from room to room, wondering if she'd ever be able to erase Rich's presence. A part of her longed to chase him out of her life, run after him militantly waving a broom, demanding he leave her alone.

Another part of her hungered to run toward him, greeting him with open arms.

"This is what happens when you fall in love," she chastised herself loudly. She pressed her hand over her smooth, flat stomach and a smile settled on her lips.

Things were different this time because a child was involved. This time she'd walk away from the relationship with a bonus. A very special bonus.

Making herself a cup of tea, Jamie sat in her kitchen, nursing her hot drink and her wounded heart. The damp tissues had piled up, but she'd composed herself enough to realize her display of anger had been out of character. No doubt Rich had viewed it as totally irrational. When she spoke to him again—*if* she did—she intended to set matters straight.

Pretense was unacceptable and she'd make sure Rich understood that.

There was a noise from her door. Since Jamie always kept it locked, she dashed into the living room, surprised to see it swing open. Rich, tall and ominous, entered her condo. He was supposed to be at work! In fact, she'd suspected he wouldn't show up at all tonight, considering the way they'd parted. One brief glance at the dark, brooding anger shining from his eyes, the tightly clenched jaw, told her he was in a furious mood.

Another surprise—the suitcase he held. It was large and bulky, the kind you'd take on an extended vacation. A three-week European tour. A two-week cruise. No one would confuse it with an overnight bag.

He set it down with a thud and headed toward her. Wide-eyed, Jamie moved out of his way.

"What are you doing here?" A challenge might not be the smartest way to start their conversation, but it told him she refused to be intimidated. He could rant and rave all he wanted, but she wouldn't be browbeaten.

"I'm here because I live here." He said it with enough conviction to make the windows vibrate. "Furthermore, I'll be sleeping in the master bedroom—with you. Is that understood?"

Coward that she was, Jamie nodded. She'd never seen Rich like this. Generally, he treated every situation in a joking manner. He could bluff, cajole and tease himself through just about anything. Jamie already knew what he'd be like when she was in labor. He'd be at her side telling jokes, entertaining the nurses, sharing good-ol'-boy remarks with Dr. Fullerton.

"No arguments?" He sounded shocked that she wasn't going to fight him over the issue of living with her, sleeping with her. Despite her contradictory emotions, she wanted him there. She wanted him in her life more than she didn't, if that made any sense.

She shook her head.

"Good." He nodded once as if to say this was going to be easier than he'd expected. "Now please explain what I said that was so despicable, when you left my office."

Jamie found it difficult to speak. "Darling."

"Yes?"

"You called me *darling,*" she said, hating that she had to explain it. She clenched her fists, her long nails digging deep into the tender flesh of her palms.

"So?" He frowned, genuinely bewildered.

"So…I'd rather you didn't." A lump was forming in her throat, but Jamie tried to ignore it.

Rich stalked to the far end of her kitchen, his back toward her. He leaned against the sink, hanging his head as if her words demanded deep concentration. After a moment he turned to face her. "You're sure it doesn't have anything to do with me working overtime?"

"Of course not," Jamie said. "That would be unreasonable."

"And objecting to being called *darling* isn't?"

Jamie lowered her gaze to the polished kitchen floor. "I...wouldn't care if you'd meant it. But we both know you didn't and worse than that—"

"Worse? You mean there's something worse than calling one's wife *darling?* Does the FBI know about this?"

"Being funny isn't going to help you this time, Rich Manning." She'd known it would be impossible to talk to him. He turned everything into a joke.

"All right," he said, lowering his voice. "Tell me what other horrible felony I've committed."

"It was the way you looked." To illustrate her point, she crossed her eyes and let her tongue dangle from the corner of her mouth.

"I looked like *that?*" he challenged in disbelief. "Don't be ridiculous!"

"Not exactly like that, but close." She held herself stiff.

"What was that silly expression supposed to be?"

"You with a besotted look."

"*Besotted?* Who uses a word like *besotted?*" He gave a short, abrupt laugh.

"I do. And I wasn't trying to be cute."

"I never looked like that in my life." Rich walked over to the round oak table, then frowned when he saw the pile of tissues. "You've been crying?"

"I…I have a cold."

He shook his head. "I thought you were never going to cry over another man."

"I…I didn't intend to…. I probably wouldn't, either, but I'm pregnant and, like you said, my hormones are all screwed up, so don't take it personally."

"What's happened to us?" He advanced several steps toward her, stopping just short of taking her in his arms. "Jamie, love…"

"Don't say that!" she cried, her voice rising to near-hysteria. Calling her his love was too painful, like taunting her with the one thing she truly wanted and couldn't have.

"What?" He raised his hands, palms up, in sheer frustration.

"Don't call me your love."

"Why?" he demanded.

"Because I'm not."

"What do you mean?" Rich glared at her.

"You don't love me and I...I can't tolerate it when you pretend you do." The words poured out of her until she was shouting, shaking with the force of her anger.

"I do love you," he said quietly.

"Oh...right." She wouldn't have thought Rich would lie to her about something so serious. It offended her that he'd try to pass off as truth what she knew to be false.

"You mean you honestly didn't realize that?" He came forward, but for every step he took, Jamie retreated two.

"Because it isn't true!"

"How can you say that after the other night?"

"Don't confuse good sex with love." Jamie didn't know what had made her say that, but she couldn't stop. She wore her pride like a protective cloak. She'd been hurt so many times before. Her trust had been violated, her heart bruised. She couldn't go through all of that again, especially with Rich, whom she loved so desperately. It was safer if he believed she didn't care.

"So that's all it was to you—good sex?"

"Yes, of course. *You* don't think it was anything more, do you?"

With each word she threw at him, his anger increased until it flashed like fire from his eyes.

Jamie's back was flattened against the wall, her fingers splayed against it. She longed to tell him their times together had been the most beautiful, the most meaningful, of her life, but she lacked the strength.

She'd never known how exhausting it was to lie.

"I suppose you want me to prove it," he said.

"Yes," Jamie returned flippantly, since that was an impossible task.

Not meeting her eyes, Rich marched past her with purposeful strides. He slammed his suitcase onto the floor, opened it and dug through his clothes until he found what he wanted—apparently a white business envelope with some kind of logo on the upper left side.

Without a word he stepped over to her fireplace, reached for one of the long-stemmed matches she kept on the mantel and struck it against the brick. The flame sprang to life.

Cupping his hand over it, Rich knelt and held the match to the white envelope, which he'd set on the grate. Within seconds the paper was nothing more than charred ashes.

At first Jamie didn't understand what he was doing. It came to her gradually, until each breath she drew was more painful than the one before. Rich had burned the marriage agreement they'd had drawn up before the wedding. The one they'd both signed.

The tears that crowded her throat refused to be contained anymore. They leapt to her eyes, burning, smarting. Her throat ached with the need to breathe, her sobs desperate to escape.

She must've made some sound, because Rich, whose back was to her, turned slowly. His eyes slid to hers, until Jamie thought she'd drown in those blue depths.

Could she believe? She was afraid to hope that what he'd said was true and that he did indeed love her. Hope was so fragile, so easily shattered.

Dare she believe?

Love had always been so disappointing. It had stripped her of her pride, stolen her aspirations. Cheated her.

Did she dare trust her heart again?

"I'm not interested in a marriage of convenience with you any longer, Jamie," he said evenly. "I haven't been, since the night I found you with Floyd what's-his-face. I realized then that I love you and probably have for years, only I hadn't realized it. Condemn me if you will, but it's the truth."

Jamie's heart quickened. Tears streamed down her face and she brought her fingers to her lips, knowing it would be impossible to speak. Instead, she held out her hand to him, her shoulders trembling.

Rich was there a second later, hauling her into his arms. His mouth unerringly found hers, and he lavished warm, moist kisses on her quivering lips.

"I hope all this emotion means what I think it does," he murmured against the curve of her neck.

Jamie's tears fell without restraint. The emotions within her were too primitive, too deeply rooted to allow her the luxury of responding with words. Her hands framed his face as she spread eager kisses wherever she could. Trying to convey everything in her heart, she cherished him with her lips, kissing him again and again until they both shook with passion.

"Jamie..." Rich tore his mouth from hers and stared searchingly into her face.

"I love you," she managed in a breathless whisper.

His smile was more brilliant than a rainbow after the fiercest storm. "I know." He wore a cocky grin as he swung her effortlessly into his arms and walked to the bedroom.

Tenderly he placed her on the bed and moved over her. When he kissed her, their passion flared to life, with no reservations, no holding back.

"Tell me what you said wasn't true," he pleaded. "Tell me our lovemaking touched you the same as it did me."

Jamie tried to answer him, reassure him it had been her pain talking, her disillusionment, but she couldn't speak for the lump in her throat. Smiling, she gazed up at him, letting all the love in her heart spill into her eyes. She wrapped her arms around his neck and kissed him.

They made love gently, slowly, and when they'd finished, they held each other. For a long time neither spoke.

They kissed after a while and Rich rolled onto his back, taking her with him. His hand caressed the small of her back. "I love you," he whispered. "I love our baby, too."

"I know.... I'm sorry I doubted you."

Content, Jamie nestled against him, pressing her ear to his heart, which beat solidly in his chest. Her own heart was radiant with emotion. She'd tried to close herself off from love, but Rich had made that impossible.

His hand reached for hers. Palm to palm. Heart to heart.

And Jamie felt—finally—like the married woman she was. A wife deeply in love with her husband. A woman deeply loved by a man.

Epilogue

The brightly decorated Christmas tree stood in the corner of Rich and Jamie's spacious new living room, in front of a large bay window that overlooked Puget Sound.

Jamie sat with her swollen ankles elevated while Rich brought her in a cup of tea from the kitchen. He'd insisted on doing the dishes and Jamie hadn't argued. She was tired and crabby and impatient for their baby to be born.

"We really should take down the tree," she said. Christmas had passed several days before.

"Take down the tree?" Rich objected. "We can't do that!"

"Why not?"

"Junior wants to see it."

"Rich," Jamie muttered, her hands resting

on her protruding stomach. "I've got news for you. Junior has decided he'd rather not be born. He's hooked his foot over my ribs and says he'd rather stay right where he is."

"You're only three days past your due date."

"It feels like three months." She'd given up any hope of seeing her feet back in October.

"Can I get you anything else?" Rich asked. "A pillow? Your knitting? A book?"

"Stop being so solicitous," she snapped.

"My, my, we are a bit testy this evening."

"Don't be cute, either. I'm not in the mood for cute."

"How about adoring?"

"Maybe...but you're going to have to convince me."

"Perhaps I should try for the besotted look." He crossed his eyes and dangled his tongue out of the side of his mouth, imitating the impression she'd done of him earlier that year.

Despite her low spirits, Jamie laughed and held her arms out to him. "I love you, even if you do look like a goose."

Rich sat on the ottoman facing her. "I love you, too. I must, otherwise I wouldn't be this worried." The humor left his eyes as he leaned forward and placed his hand on her stomach. "Come out, come out, whoever you are."

"Are you really worried?" He tended to hide his anxiety behind a teasing facade, and Jamie had been so consumed by her own apprehensions that she hadn't taken the time to address Rich's.

"I'm anxious." His hands gripped hers and he raised her knuckles to his mouth and gently kissed her fingers.

"So am I! I want this baby to be born."

"I can hardly believe how much I love him already," Rich whispered, his eyes serious. "At first, the baby was something we talked about. When I learned you were pregnant I was so excited I could've walked on water. Then a few weeks later, we were living together. This summer we sold your condo and moved here. That was only the beginning of all the changes in our lives."

"I know."

"Then Junior started getting sassy, constantly moving around, letting us know he was there."

"He—or she," Jamie said with a grin.

"I'll never forget the first time I felt him—or her— move."

"I won't, either," Jamie said.

Rich smiled that lopsided grin of his that

never failed to disarm her. "Everything's changed, hasn't it?" Once again his blue eyes brightened. "This child is part of you and me—the very best part of us both. Every time I think about him, I get all soft inside. I want to hold him in my arms and tell him how much his mother and I wanted him. Or her," he added with a smile. "Enough to go to exorbitant measures."

"Not that it was necessary," Jamie whispered. "Might I remind you that Junior was conceived in the good old-fashioned way?"

Rich leaned forward and reminded her of some other good old-fashioned methods they'd discovered. She was laughing when she felt the first contraction. Her eyes widened and she squeezed Rich's hand.

"Jamie?"

"I think all my complaining might have done some good. Have you got the stopwatch?"

Rich paled, nodded, then rushed into their bedroom, returning with the stopwatch he'd purchased after attending their childbirth classes.

He knelt in front of her, clasping her hand. "Are you ready, my love?"

Jamie nodded. She'd been ready for this moment for the past nine months.

* * *

With a loud squall, Bethany Marie Manning made her way into the world thirteen hours later. Rich was at Jamie's side in the delivery room. When Dr. Fullerton announced that they had a daughter, Rich looked at Jamie, his face filled with wonder and surprise.

"She's a girl?" he asked, as though he wasn't sure he'd heard correctly.

"Do you want to check for yourself?" Dr. Fullerton teased.

Jamie watched her husband, searching for signs of disappointment, but if there were any she didn't see them. The nurse weighed Bethany, then wrapped the protesting infant in a warm blanket and handed her to Rich.

Rich stared down at the bright pink face and smiled. When he looked over at Jamie his eyes shone with unshed tears. "She's beautiful."

"You're not disappointed we didn't have a son?"

"Are you crazy? I always wanted a girl. I just said I wanted a boy to keep you off guard." Very gently, Rich bent down and kissed his daughter's forehead.

Hours later, Jamie woke and saw that Rich was asleep, slumped in the chair next to her hospital bed. His head rested against hers. Smiling contentedly, she rubbed her fingers through his tangled hair.

Yawning, Rich raised his head. "Hello, little mother."

"Hello, proud daddy."

"She is so beautiful. Oh, Jamie, I can't believe how much I love her. And you." He kissed her hand, then held it against his jaw. "I never knew I could feel like this."

Feeling dreamy and tired, Jamie nodded and let her eyes drift shut.

"Don't you worry about a thing," Rich whispered, his face close to hers. "I've taken care of everything."

Jamie's eyes flew open. "What do you mean by that?"

"Ballet classes." He pulled open the drawer in the bedside table and withdrew a Seattle phone book. "I've called two schools, both of whom are sending us brochures. I also talked to a teacher about piano lessons."

"Rich!"

"Just kidding." He lifted her hand and clasped it between his own. "I love you, Jamie."

"I love you, too," she whispered.

They'd come so far, Jamie mused. They'd

tried to manipulate fate, create their own destiny, constrain their marriage with limits and conditions.

Instead, love had caught them unawares.

* * * * *

The ESSENTIAL COLLECTION

YES! Please send me the *Essential Collection by Debbie Macomber* in Larger Print. This collection begins with 3 FREE books and 2 FREE gifts in the first shipment, and more free gifts will follow! My books will arrive in 8 monthly shipments until I have the entire 51-book *Essential Collection by Debbie Macomber*. I will receive 2 or 3 FREE books in each shipment and I will pay just $4.99 U.S./$5.89 CDN. for each of the other 4 books in each shipment, plus $2.99 for shipping and handling. *If I decide to keep the entire collection, I'll have paid for only 32 books because 19 books are FREE! I understand that by accepting the 3 free books and gifts places me under no obligation to buy anything. I can always return a shipment and cancel at any time. My free books and gifts are mine to keep no matter what I decide.

261 HCN 1446   461 HCN 1446

Name _____ (PLEASE PRINT) _____

Address _____ Apt. # _____

City _____ State/Prov. _____ Zip/Postal Code _____

Signature (if under 18, a parent or guardian must sign)

Mail to the Harlequin® Reader Service:
IN U.S.A.: P.O. Box 1867, Buffalo, NY 14240-1867
IN CANADA: P.O. Box 609, Fort Erie, Ontario L2A 5X3

* Terms and prices subject to change without notice. Prices do not include applicable taxes. Sales tax applicable in N.Y. Canadian residents will be charged applicable taxes. This offer is limited to one order per household. All orders subject to approval. Credit or debit balances in a customer's account(s) may be offset by any other outstanding balance owed by or to the customer. Please allow 4 to 6 weeks for delivery. Offer available while quantities last. Offer not available to Quebec residents.

EDMBPA14